Grim
Brothers

Grim
Brothers

EM MCDERMOTT

Embolden Books

GRIM BROTHERS

Cover Design by GetCovers.

Published in the United States by Embolden Books.

Embolden Books
PO Box 434
Greenville, NY 12083
www.emboldenbooks.com

ISBN: 978-1-7322526-5-3 (paperback)
ISBN: 978-1-7322526-4-6 (ebook)

First Edition: December 2022

ALSO BY EM MCDERMOTT

Cursed Woods

The Woods (A Cursed Woods novel)

The Winter Stags (A Cursed Woods short story)

Other Books By Em McDermott

Asher's Gifts

CHAPTER 1

WHEN I WAS a boy, I lived in a village called Baneswood. It was peaceful then, except below the surface, where tensions simmered like bubbles roiling, about to pop.

The tensions took the form of wolves and outsiders. The mayor publicized a monthly market far and wide, and people came. They came through the woods from the village of Sleepy Bramsville, six days ride away. They came from Castle Highland, and even from the moors, where it was said there were mermaids. Some of them, seeing the quaintness of our tiny town, tasting the fresh clean air and adoring the way the close-packed trees brushed your shoulder to say hello as you walked down the road, even decided to stay. After market day, they left and returned with wagons packed full of their families. They built cottages and became neighbors. Little by little, our tiny village grew. Some of us, who did not like newness, looked into the future and saw people coming like a wave to wipe away the village we'd always known and leave behind something unfamiliar.

"They're good," "They're bad," "We're here," the voices of the town argued. But at least we could all agree on one thing: The wolves that had come with the newcomers were bad.

Perhaps the wagons trailing scraps of food had attracted them or perhaps it was simply bad luck, but a pack had taken up residence in the woods surrounding Baneswood. They were killing Marius' sheep. Worse, they hurt a girl who snuck out of her cottage after bedtime. At that news, my brother Ulf raged and shook, and the white scars on his arm—an old injury— stood out. He went to the mayor's that very minute and pounded on her door with his big fist, demanding that something be done.

So the mayor had called a town meeting to discuss the problem. All the town would be there, but it was not for hours yet. For now, the early morning sun was a yellow flower in the spring sky.

I lay on the mulch of the earth and watched spring buds and pine needles wave. Close but out of sight, a baby gurgled a laugh. I looked over to meet the grin of my niece, Greta. It was one of those wide-open smiles that only children have, utterly guileless.

"La la la," she said. She sat but wavered and might fall over. If she did, she would cry, and soon stop and begin laughing again. Tiny fists banged an invisible drum and her feet kicked nothing.

"Yes," I said, just to agree. That was the role of a good uncle.

Behind me, my two favorite women spoke to each other in low voices. I rolled over onto my stomach, and the world changed from sky and branches to thick trunks and gnarled bushes. There they were, my best friend Cat, and my younger sister Aurora. Aurora knelt below a bush, the white apron she wore stained red from the juice of the berries she picked. Her fingers were red too. She deposited her handful in a metal bucket, and used her wrist to brush a wisp of hair from her face. Her blond hair, caught back in a practical braid, shimmered in the sunlight.

Cat stood over her. Cat's shirt was sleeveless and a black tattoo stood out on her upper arm. A tree with roots that reached deep into the earth and then came up and around to become the branches. The circle of life. Nearby, her bow rested with her quiver against a tree trunk. She wore her long brown hair in a braid, but leather pants lay below her own white apron instead of a skirt. She frowned in concentration and peered at a berry, then shook her head and dropped it to the ground.

The berries with the red dots were poisonous. They thrived in the forest just alongside the blue berries with no dots at all. Animals and humans both learned young that to eat the berries with the red dots meant death. To even pick them, explode their juices on your fingers, and lick your fingers could take you near to the edge.

But the red-dotted berries made a red dye unlike any other ever seen. Aurora had discovered it just last year, and red clothes had sprung up in the village in the time since. She sold her potion to the varnisher and no one else, and not a soul but Cat and I knew how she made it.

Try to use strawberries, or raspberries, or flower petals, and the dye would be weak and watery, enough to tilt a fabric towards pinkness but not enough to bring to it that red as red as blood, that orange as vivid as sunset. Only the red-dotted berries could do that.

"Seems a shame," Cat said to Aurora, dropping another perfectly good blue berry onto the ground. "Ulf bakes such pies."

"We have the juice all over our fingers. It's not safe, not even if we wash them."

"I know, I know," Cat said, not crossly. She looked more closely at a berry before she plucked it, not wishing to create waste.

"It's been over an hour," I called to them. "Aren't you done?"

"Umph," agreed my nine-month-old niece, Greta.

"Rune, I need a lot if I'm to make a batch of dye," Aurora called back. "You could help, you know."

I grinned and sat up, gathering Greta onto my lap instead.

"Is she okay?" Aurora looked over anxiously.

"Of course. I'm going to read her a story."

I had a book with me, as I always did. It was not a children's book, but I didn't really read it. Instead, in a low voice, I summarized, making up details and telling them in an storyteller's voice, with exaggerated hand movements. Greta watched, entranced, and then I smelled something awful.

"Ugh." I lifted her off my lap and back onto the ground. "She needs to be changed."

Aurora sighed, but she pressed her hands to the dirt to rise and went to the stream to wash them so thoroughly, I half-thought she'd forgotten us. When she came back, the red color had nearly faded from her fingers, or perhaps it had faded entirely and it was only the chill of the cold stream that made her fingers red now. She changed her daughter's diaper as I read my book. She kissed Greta, settled her, and then went back to picking berries.

When the buckets were full, Cat and Aurora moved to the stream. Working in batches, they added water to the berries and crushed them until the buckets were filled with liquid red as blood. Aurora retrieved vials from a pack, and they filled and stoppered them. When they were done, they shed their aprons and washed their hands, washed and washed, and the buckets too, though Aurora insisted they never be used for anything else but this. They rinsed the vials even, and only then did they come back smiling and tired.

Aurora scooped up her daughter and made silly sounds to make her laugh. Aurora's face was red but pleased. "Dora will buy all that in a heartbeat," she said. "It'll buy Greta new shoes."

I had no idea why a baby who could not yet walk needed shoes, but I did not ask. "You'd get so much more if you sold it at the market," I said.

Aurora looked at me sternly. Her thick eyebrows made her look so much like Gus when she did this, overbearing, a smaller version of our towering older brother. "Rune, you know how dangerous this stuff is. You know that a single spotted berry can kill. This dye I make—it might as well be poison. Dora understands the danger, and I trust her to take the proper precautions, but no one else. Not another soul."

I blew out a breath. She was right, and I knew it. But still I thought of the coffers at home, and how empty they were, and Greta was another mouth to feed. "Then you could dye fabrics yourself to sell at market. Right now, Dora's making more off your creation than you are."

Aurora tickled Greta, and hugged her close. "Who has time?"

But I knew that wasn't the real reason. Her heart just wasn't in it, that's all. Aurora cared nothing for money. She cared for Greta and enjoyed potion-making. She spent her days gathering supplies from the free resources of the woods. She crushed herbs and sold simple teas and mixes for poultices and to treat colds. She made her dyes and sold them to Dora.

I looked at Cat, who'd stayed silent. She drank from a canteen and stood against a tree, not sitting like the rest of us. Her lean muscles were taut, and she peered into the woods as if on alert, but this was her version of relaxed.

I concocted a brilliant idea. "Cat could dye the fabrics. You could split the money you make."

Cat looked down, surprised but pleased. She was a huntress by trade and no washer woman, but her father was the town shepherd and she'd dyed his wools for years. Aurora trusted her more than anyone in the world, besides family, and I knew Cat could use the money too.

Aurora peered up at our friend, eyebrow raised.

"Not sure," Cat said. "I only dye wool. Dora's been selling linens."

"Wool or not, it's not a terrible idea. Here." Aurora dug into her pack and retrieved four stoppered vials. "Keep some. I'll sell the rest to Dora. You can play around with these, if you want, and after you do, you can let me know."

Cat was still hesitant. Perhaps she thought how dangerous a vat of the stuff would be. On the skin, harmless.

But allow a single drop to touch your tongue and death, instant death.

"I know," I said.

"What?" Cat asked.

"Here's what you do, Cat. Make *me* something with it. Whatever you like. If you enjoy yourself, you can make more things. If you don't, I'll have something truly special and one-of-a-kind." This would take Cat's mind off selling, and I would certainly value the present from my oldest friend. "My birthday is next month," I reminded her.

Cat laughed and rolled her eyes. "Fine, Rune. I'll give it a try. I hope you're prepared to wear a lumpy scarf, because if I make it and you don't wear it—"

Aurora leaned forward to pass up the vials. It was in this moment, as Aurora held the vials up towards Cat, that I heard a rustling in the trees. I turned my head to the sound. Cat had her bow drawn and aimed before I even settled on the source.

It was a man. He watched us from the other side of the berry grove, hiding himself within the bushes. How long had he stood watching?

His eyes were yellow, like an animal's. They fixed on the red vials that Aurora had let fall to her lap. "Careful with those," he said quietly. Almost purring, almost sensual. "Dangerous stuff you have there. And around a child, too."

Aurora's face reddened, and my heartbeat sped up in anger. She couldn't have been more careful around Greta.

"Where is it you're headed, sir?" I asked. I stood from the ground, and brushed fallen pine off my pants. I was a tall young man, though thin, and I looked down at the older man. "Perhaps I can help you on your way."

The man's eyes removed themselves from my sister and came to me. For a moment, I thought I saw anger flare, but then it was gone. He stepped forward out of the shelter of the bushes.

He wore clothing brighter than any I'd ever seen. A yellow overcoat matched his eyes. It sported blue embroidery, tassels, and ornately carved wooden buttons. I wondered if he was a prince, for I'd never seen anyone dressed as he was. Over his jacket he wore a simple leather cord around his neck. A large black animal tooth hung from it in the center of his chest. His hair was brown and beginning to thin at the peak of his head. He wore it long, the waves falling to his shoulders.

"Ah, yes. That would be very kind. I am traveling to Baneswood to sell at the market there." He raised a square case. It was wooden and leather, old and weathered, with a heavy lock to hold it shut. He had a pack across his shoulders, but no cart. He must not have come from very far if this was all he carried.

"That way." I pointed towards our village. "Not far at all. You'll pass a pasture full of sheep—" That was Cat's home, on the very edge of the town, practically in the woods themselves. "Soon after you'll see a road, and you can follow it to the square."

The stranger mimed the removal of a hat, though he did not wear one. He executed a small bow. "You have my gratitude," he said. His eyes lingered on Aurora for just another moment. She'd tucked the vials away, out of sight, and her attention was on her daughter.

"Goodbye," I said.

CHAPTER 2

"COME ON, RUNE. We're going to be late."

"Why rush on such a fine day?" I said, mostly to needle Cat. I carried Greta, and I bounced her with each step and spun her around to make her laugh and scream while Cat walked ahead of us, looking back with a frown. "Your father is quite capable of speaking for himself," I added. Cat's father, the old shepherd Marius, had been looking forward eagerly to this town meeting.

"I hope so. We need the town's help. Three sheep were killed by the pack just this week, and four last week. We can't go on like this." There was real worry in Cat's voice. I'd made her take the vials after the stranger left, for I knew she could use the money now more than ever.

"They'll put together a hunt. They'll drive them off," I assured her.

"They better." Cat's jaw was set. Determination hardened her eyes, but I could see how tired she was. She'd taken to staying up at night to watch her father's flock, bow in hand.

After four nights with little sleep, her hand had slipped as she skinned a rabbit and she'd cut herself. Marius had insisted she take a night off, and as she slept, three sheep were killed. Now she marched to this meeting as if into battle.

The mayor held the meeting in the one-room building that served as our church and school. Marius held the floor as we entered.

"I am an old man," he was saying. "I cannot sit awake all night and watch my flock. I cannot afford to hire men for this task, and my daughter can't do it alone." The old shepherd's eyes pleaded with the villagers. "The wolves must be driven away or killed!"

I handed Aurora back her daughter and hopped up to sit in a window. Greta began to fuss, attracting glowering looks from the crowd, and Aurora slipped outside. Cat stationed herself at her father's side, her chin high.

"I'll watch your flocks at night, Marius," my brother Dag offered.

"I offer my help as well," said the baker, John, who was a relative newcomer, having only moved here last year with his wife and child. "I am happy to spend what hours I can in your fields."

Marius inclined his head stiffly at the baker. Clearly one of the volunteers was more to his liking than the other.

"Fuck watching sheep," said Dag's twin, Gus. He stood in a corner, for he was too big for one of the tight pews. Our oldest brother Ulf stood beside him, and together they made the room look small. "Let's hunt."

Dag was a hunter. In the years since Cat came of age, they'd grown close and often set traps together. They even wore the same tattoo on their arm. But Dag's twin Gus was a butcher; he helped our father in his trade. He could lift a deer onto a table with barely a thought. His solutions to problems were always physical.

Beside, him, our oldest brother, Ulf, said nothing. I was surprised he was even here. Big breaths huffed in and out from his broad chest, and he stared straight ahead as if loathe to meet the eyes of the villagers who all looked at him. He was the biggest man in the village and a woodcutter, but deep scars stood out on the exposed skin of his arms. When he was a child, and exploring freely in the woods, he'd stumbled on a wolf bitch and her pups, and she'd attacked him. He'd nearly died and had been terrified of wolves ever since.

Seeing this, Dag rose from his seat and went to stand with Ulf. He did not touch him outright with his hand but stood close enough so that the bare skin of their arms was touching. It was a sign of camaraderie—family before all.

"Make up a hunting party and I'll join it," Dag said, and all the village turned their gazes off Ulf and onto Dag. "Until that can be done, I'll keep watch over Marius' flock. So that's settled."

Mayor Edda spoke. "I think the building of a fence must be considered."

Voices rose up in opposition, and the mayor frowned. For several years, she'd advocated the building of a border fence. Sleepy Bramsville had one, and the people who came from there talked at length of its virtues.

"We do not need a fence," I spoke up, "unless it is to keep out all the newcomers who we now welcome to our market. Besides, where would those with houses in the woods fall?

Would you lock them outside the village that has always been their home?"

"Of course not! The fence could circle around all the homes in the outskirts."

"And my sheep would graze inside this fence?" Marius asked. His tone was skeptical, but I thought that he was just a little bit intrigued.

"Where would we get the money for something like that?" asked Arne, the cobbler.

"Why, the woods offer free supplies! We could fell timber, the same as any of you would to build a fence around a garden," Mayor Edda suggested.

"Yes, the woods provide so much, let's cut ourselves off from them," I muttered.

The varnisher, Dora, always a wise woman, spoke up. "Let's put together a hunting party. In the meantime, we'll be careful not to go out at night, and Dag and John can watch Marius' flocks. As for money, the market has been drawing in many folks from outside the village. Perhaps in a few months, we can reassess."

Everyone agreed. No hasty solutions; no resolutions or decisions of permanence. The mayor took credit for the growth of the monthly market, which was opening very soon indeed, and we must all get to work now, mustn't we?

We drifted out of the church as the bell above our heads rang for no reason at all. One child's over-enthusiasm, and the bell keeper's willingness to indulge.

CHAPTER 3

"So we'll have a hunt," Gus said cheerfully. His arms swung at his sides as he took big steps towards our butcher shop.

Ulf scowled beside him and took larger steps to walk ahead. He did not notice as a child, not looking, ran into his leg and tripped. Ulf glowered down at him, and stepped around the fallen boy.

I sidled up to Gus. "You know the thought of a hunt scares Ulf. You could be a little considerate of that."

Gus frowned in confusion. "Rune, what better way to keep safe from wolves than to kill them when they get close?"

I sighed. Ulf's fear had never made sense to Gus, who had been there that day too. He was so small he could do nothing to help as he watched his older brother torn apart. The experience that had seeded Ulf's fear had put in Gus a stubborn resolve to *do something* whenever possible.

Dag reached the fallen child. He bent down and smiled. "Ut-oh," he said. "You okay?"

The child, a boy named Bragi, grinned. One of his front

teeth was missing, and one was only half grown in. "Yeah. But I've gotta get going. The sprites only give you coin if you leave your gift before noon." He opened his palm to display a lost tooth, still pink with blood.

"Ooh," Dag said at seeing the disgusting artifact. "You better hurry then." He held out his hand to lift up the boy, who did not need his help at all. The boy disappeared behind us, fast as wind.

Dag laughed as he went, and looked at me. I'd stopped to peer at the tooth, but Ulf and Gus had gone ahead and could no longer hear. "We were all like that once," Dag said.

I nodded. "Do you remember Aurora? She saved all her teeth so she could bring them at once and get a pile of coin to spend on a new dress before Father could find it and spend it."

Dag remembered. Aurora had carefully hidden her efforts from our father, and he hadn't noticed her missing teeth. So it was Dag who had snuck to the grove where the sprites paid for teeth, to sprinkle her coin and collect the treasures she'd left.

"She was so proud of that dress. We could hardly get her to take it off."

"Not until she grew out of it."

"And then she had those ribbons made from it—"

"And still wears them," I finished.

Dag smiled ruefully at me. "Ah, the joys of a simple childhood, huh, Rune?" He slapped my back and continued on down the street, his lanky legs taking the steps easily, in no rush.

We arrived at the shop together. Above the door hung the sign of a butcher shop. A cleaver, like the one Gus carried in the pocket of his apron, was painted on a simple wooden board.

Beside the door, burnt into the cedar siding, was the image of the tree that Dag and Cat wore on their arms. Father had been furious when he'd first noticed it. But of course, he'd done nothing.

Aurora arrived first and held the door with Greta on her hip. The rest of us filed in, all five siblings making the shop seem small.

Gus disappeared into the cellar and came up again with a scowl.

"What is it?" Aurora asked him. She shifted Greta to the other hip.

"Today's market stuff is all still here."

Collectively, we sighed. This meant that Father, who had not attended the town meeting, had not taken his wares to the market instead. The market opened at noon, which was fast approaching. Now the work fell to us.

"I'll check the house," Dag said, ever the optimist. We all knew he was not likely to be found there.

"I'll check the tavern." Ulf ducked back out the door.

"He could've at least made it to the meeting," Gus grumbled. He reached for his apron, which hung on the wall streaked with old red stains. He tied it around his waist.

"I'll pack up," Aurora assured Gus. "You get started with what you meant to do today."

Gus nodded. But even as she offered to help him in his work, there was a stiffness to his gratitude, as if the fight they had when she became pregnant with Greta still hung between them. I could hear it in my memory, the cruel screaming words he'd hurled at her. Her calm determination. Yes, she was young to have a child, she'd said to him. Yes, she'd been unwise with that boy and now would have to do this alone.

"You're not alone," Dag had reminded her, his tone a subtle scolding of his twin, even though he said nothing direct to condemn him. "You have all of us."

"And anyway, I've been taking care of this family for years," Aurora had reminded Gus, raising her chin in the air. "I think I can handle a child." And she had and she did.

Gus disappeared into the back room where the meat waited for his cleaver and carving knife.

Aurora made for the stairs to the cellar, but she turned back. "Rune, will you go with Ulf? He'll have too much trouble getting Father home alone."

"You don't want my help packing up?"

"Dag'll be back in a minute. He'll help me."

"Sure," I said.

The bell rang as I went out our door and took quick light steps across the dirt street towards the tavern that, by rights, shouldn't even have been open.

I opened the door and a bell rang just like ours. The barkeep Miranda looked up as I entered and snorted. "Come to take my customers away? Least you could do is buy a beer."

"He buys enough beers," I said sourly. I did not like Miranda, who leaned over our father with her large bosom, trying to become his fourth wife. Why she'd ever want that honor, I could not imagine.

Our father married Ulf's mother young. They were barely more than kids when she died having Ulf, and our father quickly married again. His second wife was an evil woman. Cruel. She gave birth to twins, Gus and Dag, and then to me. I was too young to fall victim to her abuse, but I remembered watching her beat my brothers. My father, a longtime drunk, did little to stop it until one day when she went too far and broke Dag's arm. Ulf and Gus, both just boys, joined together and ran her off. Father was furious, though it didn't take him long to find Aurora's mother. She was a stunning young woman who'd taken all of us under her wing. She nearly sobered our father up, but when she died of a sudden sickness, he went back into the bottle again.

Ulf sat at the counter drinking a beer beside our father's snoring form. I sat on Father's other side and said nothing, just waited for Ulf to finish.

Ulf threw back the dregs and sighed. He stood. "Ready?"

I nodded. Ignoring the over-sweet scent of cloves and fermentation, we threw our father's arms around our shoulders and walked him out. The toes of his boots dragged along the ground. This happened so often that Aurora had sewn extra leather there, so that he would not have toes sticking out. We dragged him through the streets, shame burning our faces as villagers saw us and shook their heads. The strangers here for market day were the hardest, for they stared instead of looking away.

I reached out awkwardly for our shop door and threw it wide. It banged against the wall and we lifted Father's toes over the lip and up into the shop. I heard Cat's voice as we came in. "Oh, only I thought I'd find your father at market. My father sent me to speak with him regarding an inconsistency with the last payment we received."

Gus's apron was bloody, and his fingers were too. He held them spread out wide so that he would remember not to touch anything. He closed his eyes, pinched them shut, and took a deep breath and let it out. He opened them and refocused on Cat. "What's the inconsistency?"

"We were paid for five lambs, but we sent ten." Gus took deep breaths as Cat fished into her pocket. "I'm sorry, Gus. I have Father's records. He only asked me to compare against yours…"

Gus's shoulders were stiff. "Cat, I'll be frank with you. I doubt my father wrote it down right. I'll take Marius at his word and get you the payment. But right now I just *need* to get to market or I won't have the money to pay you."

"Of course!" Cat was flustered and apologetic. "How can I help?"

"Does this mean you're closed?" a new voice said. A stranger had followed us through the door and now stepped around us and out into the open. Gus had not seen him come in, and would never have been so honest with Cat if he had. His eyes narrowed and the stranger's mouth curved up, subtle and unpleasant. His teeth were strangely pointed. His eyes roved over my father's lightly snoring form, up and down, watching the drool that dripped from his mouth onto the shop floor. They laughed up at Gus, who stood with his chest puffed out and his cheeks red. The eyes were a strange yellow color, like piss in snow.

It was the stranger from the forest.

"Yes. You can find us at the market," Gus said stiffly.

"Ah, but apparently not!" the stranger pointed out. He laughed out loud, as if this was all very funny indeed. "Though," he looked at our father, scenting the reason for his state, "it is still *awfully* early."

Ulf glared him down. The stranger was not tall and Ulf

towered over him, and yet he looked mildly up at Ulf as if he were not at all alarmed by the giant before him. "Maybe too early to buy meat then," Ulf said moodily. "Maybe come back later."

"Ah, but I fancy some ham for luncheon," said the man, jovial, as if he had a lovely picnic planned.

"We'll be at the market before luncheon," Gus said stiffly. "You can buy ham from us then."

"Thanks for stopping by," I added. My eyes on the door suggested a path for him. Gus and Ulf were glaring, and my father was becoming heavier every moment. "Come on, Ulf. Let's get him in bed," I said.

But Ulf wouldn't take his eyes off the stranger. Something in him had gone territorial, and he would not leave the shop unprotected while this man was in it. So we stood in the door, an awkward three-man shape, while the man stood and waited.

"I'm afraid I may be gone by the time you make your way there," the stranger explained. "I am only passing through, and meant to eat my lunch in the woods on my travels."

That's not what he said this morning. He said he came to sell at the market.

But still I hoped it was true, because there was something about this man, some subtle energy, that made me hope he would not linger in our town.

"Aurora," Gus shouted.

The man jumped at the boom, then smiled at me. At first embarrassed, like any startled man, but then his look settled on my father and became mocking once more.

"Bring up some ham, will you?" Gus called.

Steps banged on the stairs and Aurora surfaced, still holding her daughter, pushing sweaty blond hair back from her face. She was slightly flushed, as if she rushed to pack the meats.

"What? Gus, I couldn't hear you."

"Ham. I need ham. How much do you want?" Gus turned to the stranger.

Only then did Aurora notice and look at him. "Oh, hello," she said. "I think we met this morning."

The stranger's face had utterly changed. He looked stricken, pale as if he'd seen a ghost. He swallowed visibly and pulled at the tall collar around his neck. He swept my sister a deep bow at the waist.

"Hello again, my lady," he said. His voice was husky, not at all silky smooth like before. "What a lovely name you have. I am very pleased to make your acquaintance. I am Igor, a humble traveling apothecary." The man flushed, as if proud of his formal speech.

I glanced over at Gus, who was staring with visible distaste. Ulf looked amused. He rolled his eyes at me and I almost laughed out loud.

"How much ham?" Gus said roughly. His voice seemed to shatter the magical moment for the stranger, who stiffened and rose, a dour expression coming back onto his face as he regarded my brother. Gus put his hands on his hips and waited.

The stranger's eyes strayed back to my sister. "Well, I was planning a humble lunch for one, but perhaps I was not ambitious enough. My lady, fate seems determined to bring us together. I admit, I expected to find you in the home of a sick woman, or perhaps in your own apothecary shop, selling your wares." He beamed as if he meant these things as compliments, and perhaps they were.

"This is my father's shop," Aurora said, her tone neutral and polite, but I saw in her eyes that she did not like him.

"I would like to meet the fellow," Igor went on, oblivious of her attempt to dismiss him. "He must be wonderful, having raised such a daughter."

Had he so quickly forgotten his insults for the man before him?

Gus harrumphed from behind the counter.

"If you'll excuse me," Aurora said, "it's market day, and I have a lot of work to get to."

Igor leapt forward. "Oh, let me help you! I am eager to see and do things in this town, for I might stay."

But he just said he was leaving shortly.

Aurora opened her mouth to answer, but before she could, our father snorted and raised his head. We all looked at him in surprise. He wore his apron, as if he'd meant to come to work after all. The once-white fabric was smeared with blood and other fluids, and a smell like viscous organs and old beer emanated from him. He sniffled and wiped his nose with the edge of his palm. His hair was flat on one side and standing up on the other. His eyes blinked like it was a little bit too bright.

"That's the damn problem with this town now," he said, slurring. I wondered how long he'd been partly awake, head down, listening. "Damn foreigners come—comin' in. Gotta wake up at dawn's ass crack to go talk about it!" He snorted and coughed.

He had no idea what time it was, I realized. He thought the meeting hadn't happened yet. He'd probably started drinking last night.

Igor's expression had soured, as if he held a lemon in his

mouth. He pulled down his coat at his waist and puffed out his chest. His eyes were like a fire's dancing flame, one moment enraged, the next hurt, the next calculating. "Well. I will say good day for now, my good lady." He addressed Aurora only, giving her a stiff and formal bow. Clutching his wooden case close to his side, he hurried out the door. The bell rang behind him as he closed it.

"That was rude," I said, once he'd left. "He's still a customer, if nothing else."

Our father said nothing. His head fell again to his chest as if, having run off the stranger, he'd done his job and now went to rest. But I was really addressing Gus, who'd been hardly better.

Aurora shivered and looked at the closed door with a faraway expression on her face. She soothed Greta, though the child was not fussing. "I don't know, Rune. There's something about him. He's...wrong." Aurora made a silly face at her daughter, then wiped drool from Greta's chin. "I can't explain it. I just feel it."

Gus wasn't listening. He had wiped off his hands and was bowed over the paperwork Cat had asked for, a deep frown on his face. She waited in a corner, saying nothing about the whole exchange.

"Gus," I called him. "Gus."

"Huh?" He looked up at his name.

"Aurora says she . gets a bad feeling around the new stranger."

Gus huffed and shuffled the papers. "Bad feeling or not, we shouldn't run off customers. We need 'em." Still frowning, he opened our money box, handed coins to Cat, and disappeared into the back room without a word. He seemed to have forgotten that he himself had just insulted the man to his face. But then, it had become a habit for him to never agree with Aurora.

I shook my head. Igor might be hoping to stay, but he certainly had not earned a very warm welcome.

CHAPTER 4

As a child I hid in the trees that shadowed the dirt paths that provided bumpy passage for merchant's carts on market day. One particular pothole was my favorite. When fruit and other goodies flew off the carts and the merchants went on, swearing, I'd shimmy down the tree to grab my prize, then back up again to place it into Cat's hands.

"Half for you," I'd say.

She giggled, though it was hard for her to take the fruit when her arms were wrapped so tight around the tree. I took to climbing like a natural-born squirrel. She never had, but she followed me up the trees anyway. I'd carve off sections of the fruit with my knife and deposit them in her mouth. Juice trickled down her chin and I'd use her apron to wipe it clean.

Today was a market day like all of those ones. In a tiny village like ours, the world goes round and round. But Cat was grown now, and had sorted out the payment issue with Gus and gone on her way.

Now, late in the afternoon, I sat up in my tree with a book, letting my legs dangle on either side of the branch. Through the cover of spring foliage, I watched the merchants roll their carts to and from the town center. Every month there were more of them. The mayor had been busy laying cobbles to form a proper town square. The old hole in the path was gone, filled in, and the carts that had traveled far through the woods to get here rolled smoothly down the packed dirt.

The feeling of anonymity was leaving our tiny village. Now we were a place, six days' ride from Sleepy Bramsville and only eleven to Castle Highland. Without much thought, I hopped down from my tree and I walked towards a place that still was no place.

My steps were long now; I was a lanky young man and no longer a child. I carried nothing on my back and only a book in my hand. The trees soon swallowed the chatter of market day behind me, leaving a different kind of chatter. The chit-chat of birds and the muttering of squirrels, the rustling of deer and the laughing of creeks. The soft soothing whisper of the trees as the wind touched them. Flashes of light teased the edges of my vision as tiny winged sprites blinked in and out of the Shadow Realm. I smiled and slowed my walk. I was going nowhere, after all.

The particular nowhere place I was headed was my tree house. Well, it wasn't just mine. Fondly I remembered those days when we were all young—my three brothers, my sister, and Cat. We built it together. Strong Ulf chopped branches from trees with a hatchet he'd taken from our father when he wasn't looking. Cat designed the thing, arguing with Ulf over unnecessary intricacies. Gus carried over water from the stream so that nobody would go thirsty while I ran up and down the

tree, holding tight to pieces of wood so that Dag could nail
them in. Aurora was too little then to be much help. She
directed from the ground, and set out picnics with nuts and
berries she'd foraged as we worked.

We worked long hours, and hard, and went home covered
in sweat and smiles. I wondered how long it had been since the
others had used the tree house. I was the only one who went
there now. It seemed everybody else had grown up.

But when I approached, I heard voices. Stilling, I cast my
gaze across the ground and saw no one. It came from the trees.
A forest sprite, I thought at first, but I looked about and saw
nothing hovering in a sprite's telltale shape.

It must be people in the tree house. I crept closer, quiet, feeling
suddenly the hot surge of possessiveness.

A woman laughed, and the heat dispelled like a cool breeze
on a summer day. It was Cat. I smiled. How long it had been
since we met here? Once it happened so often. I sat up there
and read, and she stayed below, picking berries and mushrooms
and herbs from the wild. She gathered them in her apron and
when she had enough, I came down. We'd sit against the trunk
of the tree and she'd pass me her catch. I'd munch on the feast
and tell her of the story I read. Tales from far from here. Tales
of adventure. I opened my mouth to call out to her.

But before I could speak, I recognized the other voice.
Dag, my brother.

Perhaps not strange; it was his tree house too, after all. Two
hunters in the woods. Yet the tiny pea of possessiveness was
back again, and instead of calling out, I crept forward and
listened.

"You should get going," Cat said. "You'll go home with

no catch, and then what would people say?"

"They'd say I'm a bad hunter," Dag answered matter-of-factly, and Cat giggled. As always, there was an ease in his tone, a lack of worry about everything. "But they won't. I'm catching rabbits right now. I set some traps on my way here."

They kissed. I knew because the speaking stopped, and the sounds of the woods intruded and made me feel like an intruder myself. I should leave and let them have their privacy. I could not see them yet from where I stood, and I suspected that was good. My mind conjured an image of the two of them lying naked on a bed of their cloaks. Cat's basket lay on the ground below the tree.

"Well, *I* have some work I need to get to, even if you don't," she teased.

"You should go to the market and gauge the interest in your red dye. Dora's been selling like mad. People are hungry for the color. We can go together."

Cat said nothing. Maybe she shivered, or shook her head. She did not speak.

"Why not?" Dag asked.

"Dora can sell her linens to them. Maybe I'll even try dying wool; I don't know. But I won't sell the dye, and neither will your sister."

"You'd make a bigger profit—"

"No."

"But why? What are you afraid of?"

"Dag, it's not even really my decision. But I agree with Aurora completely. It's too risky. It's basically poison. I couldn't stand it if someone got hurt."

"You can warn them, Cat. Tell everyone who buys—"

"No. No, because people don't always listen. Come on, Dag, think about how you would feel if you were accidentally responsible for hurting someone."

My brother was silent, and because I knew them both so well, I knew her comment had hit home.

There wasn't much my brother Dag was afraid of. The man lay on a bed the forest had made for him. The food he ate, he trapped himself. I'd gone with him hunting sometimes, and I knew he kept his kills clean and said a prayer of thanks to the Great Stag for every spirit he took with his bow or his knife. Through the sweat of his body and the kindness of his spirit, he earned everything he needed to get by. And though he did not rely on others, they relied on him, and he never had an unkind word for anybody.

"Do you remember my mom?" Dag asked her. The ease was gone from him. The memory of our mother made the air feel cold.

"I remember when we were kids, and I'd come over to play. We'd run away from her to hide in the trees. I was never around her much."

No, Cat and I were too young to have born the brunt of my mother's cruelty. Dag, three years my senior, was just the right age. His young face had been so often yellowed, his ribs purple.

"I could never hurt someone, Cat," Dag said quietly. Did he hug her more closely as he said it? Did she put her hand on his cheek? "I could never be like her."

"Oh Dag, but you're nothing like her. You're kind and fair. You never even shout; you don't even have a temper. How could you be like her?"

"I don't know. Blood's blood, right? Sometimes, I feel something in me that scares me. Sometimes, I think…maybe one time, maybe by accident."

"You feel something like what?"

I was curious myself. A lifetime of knowing him and I'd never caught a glimpse of it. I took a careful step forward, silent, so that I could hear his quiet voice.

"Like a river eel slithering along, getting slime on everything it touches."

"I don't know what that means."

Dag sighed. I could see them now, only just. Bare shoulders and bodies wrapped in long cloaks. Dag rubbed Cat's shoulder and smiled, bringing himself out of his dark ruminations. "Just that sometimes I think there's a piece of her in me somewhere, and if the right bad thing happened, it would come out, and I could hurt somebody."

"Oh, Dag," Cat whispered, her palm on his cheek.

He rolled on top of Cat and kissed her, and I knew I had to leave. I could tell that he no longer wished to speak of this, and I did not want to witness what happened next. I felt like an intruder enough already.

"I'm just saying I do understand about the dyes," he said, before long steps took me too far away to hear more. I walked somewhere, but I did not think about where. Another nowhere place, I guess, only the thing about places is that the meaningful ones bring you back over and over. I found myself at this morning's berry grove without much surprise.

I climbed a tree and sat to read, but my eyes skimmed the words without seeing.

Dag and Cat. I hadn't known, and yet the ease with which

they touched and spoke told me they had been together for some time.

She'd chosen the kindest of us—maybe the kindest man in the village. And he was handsome, with long waves of brown hair and sweet brown eyes with long lashes. A lanky fit body with muscles through the shoulders from pulling the string of his heavy bow. Cat loved the trees, and Dag would not make her leave her father's house to come into the growing village and shout out her window to neighbors across the street. She'd made a good choice.

Yet still it unsettled me. I hadn't known that the time for those choices had come, and had I known, perhaps I might've done something other than linger in memories of childhood. I was a man of twenty now, and Cat was twenty-one, and had I known…

But even as I thought these things to myself, I knew they were not true. I loved her, yes. But she wanted a man, and I was not ready to grow up.

CHAPTER 5

MARKET DAY PASSED and the out-of-towners went back to where they came from. I watched from a tree as their carts rolled down the cobblestone path that became dirt and disappeared between the trees.

Which is why I was so surprised two days later when Igor walked once more into my father's butcher shop.

I lay on the wooden floor on my stomach. Before me sat Greta, who gurgled and giggled, rocking on her bum as her thick fingers clenched around the wooden figure of a horse I'd carved for her. Whittling was always a hobby of mine, and I was proud of the intricate detail of the horse's textured mane.

Aurora was nearby, as she always was when I watched Greta. Today she was outside behind the shop, smoking and drying meats. Gus was in the back room butchering, and I was the watcher of the shop front. Dag and Ulf were in the woods, of course, and Father was where he always was.

The bell rang. A warm breeze came in as the door opened, rustling Greta's pale curls.

"Hello," I called up, my eyes following my voice. I saw it was him, wearing the same suit of gold. As before, in one hand he clutched his briefcase.

Igor raised his eyebrows as his eyes lowered to find me. He did not lower his chin, only the gaze of his yellow eyes. "Hello. Are you open?" He sounded as if he doubted it.

"Of course," I said, jumping nimbly to my feet. "How can I help?" I was brisk and business-like.

Igor's gaze took in the mostly empty shop. Standing in jars on shelves were Aurora's dried meats, but all the fresh meat was kept in the cellar or the ice box.

"I suppose I expected to buy meat, and yet you seem to have little." He chuckled uneasily. "I'm beginning to wonder if this is truly a butcher's shop."

Was the man trying to be insulting? He seemed to come to it naturally. I wondered where he'd come from that he was so unfamiliar with the way a small shop was run.

"We have plenty, if you'll just tell me what it is you want." Now there was an edge to my voice, an unfriendliness that perhaps reminded him of the unfriendly welcome he'd found here before. He frowned, and then his face was wiped clean, and he donned a bright smile that did not reach his eyes. He strolled about the room, a finger grazing each shelf he passed as if he checked for dust. When he turned, his hair flew back from his ear and I caught a glimpse of its tip, which was pointed like his teeth.

"You know, a man might feel he's not wanted in these parts."

"Don't take it personally. We're just not much for strangers." I decided to try to be nice. "In a town so small, most of us have known each other since we were children. It must be hard to be the newcomer."

At these words of kindness, Igor's eyes swept me up and down, assessing. Perhaps he wondered if I was being genuine.

"Indeed," he said finally. "But everything comes in time, including familiarity. And familiality! In truth, I am thinking of staying. Setting up a little shop of my own, perhaps. There's a lovely new two-story for sale." He gestured out the window towards a newly built tower that my father and other old-timers had called a monstrosity. Apparently, the mayor's plan to attract out-of-towners was working.

"What is it that you sell?"

"Oh, this and that. Potions and powders to cure ailments. I'm an apothecary, you see."

I nodded, remembering that he'd mentioned this before. We lapsed back into silence for a moment. Then, at the same time, I said, "What can I get you from the back?" as he said, "Is your sister around?"

I hesitated. She was, and yet I did not wish to tell him. As if summoned by his mention of her, Aurora rounded the corner and came into sight before I could answer. The acrid smell of smoke swept into the room with her.

"I figured Greta must need changing by now—" she was saying, her eyes roving the floor for her baby. Then she looked up and saw us. Instantly her expression closed down. Her hands crossed over her chest even as she said, "Oh, hello," in as friendly a voice as ever.

The apothecary's face was a lantern of light at the sight of her. His yellow eyes became beams of sun that spilled out from within him. Aurora lifted Greta from the floor, smelling her diaper, as Igor said, "My lovely Aurora. How wonderful it is to see you again."

She nodded, smiling distantly. "Can I help you?" She kept it professional.

"Ah. Indeed. That would be most gracious." He took two steps toward her, light on his feet, almost dancing. "What is the best product you sell?"

She blinked in confusion. "I'm sorry?"

"What is your most sumptuous meat?"

Aurora's eyes darted to me as I resisted the urge to laugh at the absurd question. As ever, her answer was kind. "We just sell meat. I'm afraid that will depend on your personal preferences. Most people find pig to be quite a luxury."

"I see. Of course, of course. But what is your personal favorite?" He took another step towards her, his eyes gleaming. Eager.

She took a small step backwards, pivoting her daughter away. "I suppose I enjoy venison. My brother hunts it himself, and I like that the animal lived its life free and happy before the end."

The apothecary beamed at her. "A kind soul you are indeed. I'll take two pounds."

"I'll get it—" I started to say, but Aurora interrupted.

"No, no. I've got it. I'll be right back with it." She threw open the trapdoor and descended.

The light in the apothecary's eyes had gone out. He clutched his briefcase, his fingers white on the handle. His eyes locked on the black hole where Aurora had gone, waiting for the moment she'd come back.

I cleared my throat. "An apothecary, huh? So you cure

headaches and make healing salves? Things like that?"

"Yes, things like that," he murmured.

"Aurora is pretty good with potions too," I said, and then wanted to kick myself. It was as if his focus on her drew my own mind to her as well, as if all the air in the room was waiting for her return to breathe.

"I remember," he said, his voice still soft. Not at all full of his usual arrogance.

"You're interested in her for more than just her beauty," I observed.

This pulled his eyes from the hole in the floor. "I am," he admitted. "Will you do me a favor, my boy? You seem like a decent sort, not like your brothers."

I stiffened at that. A strange insulting compliment, especially when he'd met us all just once. But he did not wait for my affirmation to continue.

"If she ever wants to learn, you send her to me. I'd be happy to give her an apprenticeship. There's much I could teach a woman of her talent."

"I'll do that," I said, but now my voice was stiffer, for I thought of how Aurora had turned her child away from him.

Igor seemed to pick up on this. He studied my face closely and then sighed, turning back to the trapdoor.

Aurora reentered without Greta. She went right to the counter and wrote his order up. She told him the amount in a cheery, detached tone, and made sure she didn't touch his hand when he passed her the coin.

"Good day," she said as he left. The bell rang at his exit. As soon as he was gone, she shuddered. "There's just something about him, Rune. Something wrong."

She did not wait to ask for my opinion. She went back to her daughter and her work.

CHAPTER 6

THE HUNT GATHERED before dusk that evening, their faces hard, their hands clenched tight around the instruments they used to farm. Hoes and hatches and pitchforks. These folks were unused to violence.

"Sorry lot," I said to Dag.

His bow was slung over his shoulder. "They'll do. Really we're just scaring the wolves anyway." He winked and smiled, ever easy.

We waited in silence in the square as night came on. The sky purpled over the trees and the branches became black arms that reached out for a hug from the moon, which failed to appear. The air was scented with hyacinths and wisteria.

Igor arrived.

"What's he doing here?" Gus said sourly, watching his approach. He'd borrowed Ulf's axe, and his hand held it loosely. With hardly an effort, he could swing it and run a man through. But my brothers were not like that. "He said he wasn't staying in town."

"He's thinking of staying," I told Gus. "He was in the shop today. Do you know that white tower across from the baker's?"

My brothers nodded. It was a speculation project by the mayor, one more attempt to draw people to our small village. Apparently it was working, and only half the town was happy about it. I saw it in their faces as Igor approached.

"He might buy it and open a shop."

Igor carried his case in his hand. I wondered if he'd let it go once he established his shop. I'd not yet seen him without it. But he put it down when he reached the group and held out his arms as if to welcome us, even though it was he who had just arrived. "Ah, is this the hunting party?"

Nobody answered him. Of course it was.

"Marvelous. I thought I'd lend my assistance."

Snickers in the crowd. My brothers looked out at their friends, the men they'd grown up with, and they shared a private joke that was clear to all of us: that this little elven man, short, with a flamboyant yellow and red jacket, was unlikely to be of any help at all.

"Ah," Igor said, seeming to read our minds. He picked up his case and clutched it close to his chest. "But you see, I think you will be happy to have me."

We went out to Marius' fields and took up positions in tall grasses and behind low stone walls. Sheep bleated, their sleep disturbed by our presence. Igor moved with unexpected quietness through the underbrush while many others crunched and tripped on fallen branches.

The wolves probably would be alert to our presence before we even got close. If we were lucky, they'd approach near Dag or another hunter, and we might fell some. I did not see Cat in the crowd. She was one of the best shots in the village, but she'd exhausted herself lately keeping watch, and Marius had insisted she take the night off.

As for me, I'd come mostly to watch. I'd taken a knife from my father's shop in case of a close call, but I had no intention of killing anything. I had no skills to offer.

Igor, as if sensing our sameness in this regard, took up a seat beside me in the grass. He stretched his legs out and wiggled his boots back and forth, and my mind conjured the image of him picnicking alone in the woods with a slice of ham for luncheon.

"Where's your other brother?" he asked, too loudly.

Villagers frowned at us, and I clenched my jaw, disliking the subject.

"He was otherwise engaged," I answered quietly.

"I'd love to know what else might engage a woodcutter at night in a tiny village such as this one. A woman, perhaps?" Igor raised an eyebrow, and then clicked his tongue and shook his head. I got the eerie feeling he already knew the reason for Ulf's absence.

"Oh yes, I remember. I heard he's quite afraid of wolves, isn't he? Terrified. Big man like that, it's such a shame."

Yes, there was his mocking tone again. There was his sharp edge, hidden, like a knife dipped in honey.

I stared straight ahead. Igor had been in the village for only a few days and yet he knew so much about us. Nobody seemed to want to talk to him, so where did he get his information?

Igor was not one for waiting, or so it seemed. He tapped

his feet together in the grass. His boots made a low clunking sound as they touched. His eyes did not rove amongst the tree trunks looking for wolves, though perhaps his strange pointed ears could hear better than those of ordinary men.

"If I may ask," I said quietly, "how is it you came by such unusual ears?"

He grinned, and his feral pointed teeth showed in his mouth. "Ah. The cost of a spell I cast many years ago. A disturbing surprise at first, I assure you, but they've grown on me."

"A—a spell?"

His smile broadened. His teeth gleamed, although there was no moon tonight and the world was very dark. "Indeed. Not all my potions and powders are entirely what might be called natural. Some of them require energy to work."

"Are you talking about magic?" I'd read many stories over the years that featured sorcerers, and even heard tales from the mouths of out-of-towners who traded words for coin. But none with a ring of truth.

The forest was magic, of course. Towering stags guarded precious havens full of plants that could save lives. There were sentient critters no hunter would dare to shoot. Sprites who flitted like birds at dusk, lighting the sky with the fire in their wings. And even women like Aurora, who sensed those things more deeply than the rest of us. But these magics were the most natural thing in the world, and no man wielded them.

"Why, of course." Seeming without thought, Igor pet his case.

"What's in it?" I asked, suddenly incredibly curious to know.

"Perhaps you'll see," he said. "I did tell you I'd be useful. I have a particular affinity for killing wolves. I do hope I get to show off my skills."

Around his neck he wore a large black tooth. I'd noticed it the first time I met him. "Is that a wolf's tooth around your neck?"

"Indeed it is. It is the tooth of the very wolf who was responsible for my altered figure. Perhaps if we sit here long enough, I'll tell you the story—"

A howl cut the air. Igor sat up tall, instantly alert. Nearby, Dag, seasoned and calm, merely cocked his ear to hear better as inexperienced villagers exploded from the grasses, pitchforks raised.

"Sit down, goddammit," Gus hissed. "They're not close yet."

The villagers retreated back behind their stone fences to wait. At each howl, their eyes darted to the seasoned hunters. They tried to imitate their calm. Dag lounged with his bow beside him. He picked wildflowers and tore the petals off with nimble fingers, tossing them aside.

Everyone was quiet, ears pealed for the next sound.

Gradually, we heard them coming. They came quietly, so as not to spook the sheep, but we could hear the occasional crack of a stick. Their blue eyes glowed like orbs of sprite light.

Dag put a finger to his lips. He moved slowly and silently, taking his bow in his hand and an arrow from his quiver. Everyone else froze to watch. Dag nocked the arrow, but he did not draw yet.

The first wolf began to run. He raced towards a bunch of sheep, who bleated and scattered.

Chaos erupted. Villagers burst from the grasses and raced

forward screaming, hatchets held high.

Dag sighted and drew. Loosed his arrow. But the wolf had startled at the sound of the emerging villagers. Dag's arrow flew past and skittered into empty grass. "Damn it," he swore.

Gus raced towards the wolf, who was trapped in the middle of the field by a closing circle of farmers. Sheep ran about in panic. The wolf stopped and stood still, growling as the circle closed around him. He began to bark loudly, calling his pack to his aid.

Dag drew another arrow. The wolf was still, for now. If no villagers got in the way, Dag would soon put him down. But there were people moving everywhere.

"Out of the way," Dag shouted.

But at the same moment, Igor cried out: "I've got him!" His voice was a triumphant trumpet, although he'd done nothing so far but stand up.

The tabs of his case snapped open, and he reached inside with hardly a glance. He swept a vial into his hand and tossed it into the air in the direction of the wolf.

It was chaos and it was dark. Perhaps I alone watched the stoppered vial tumble end over end in a perfect toss towards the place where the wolf growled, his teeth bared, ready to defend himself against the encroaching crowd.

The contents of the vial were gold. When I watched closely, they sparkled like caught sunlight.

The vial crashed down right on the head of the wolf and shattered. There was an explosion, a massive kapow. Dirt and grass flew among bits of bloody sheep and wolf. The closest people were thrown back, Gus among them. Debris rained down on our heads as we cowered under our arms, and only

Igor stood up straight and tall, his face flushed with pride or pleasure.

Afterwards, there was dead silence. Slowly, we each blinked and dropped our arms. There was a small crater in the middle of Marius' field. There was not enough wolf left to tell there had once been a wolf, and all the sheep nearby were gone too.

Gus and several others sat just at the perimeter of the circle, touching their ears.

"By all that's unholy," the baker's wife intoned, her voice wavering. She stumbled over her feet as she fled.

Others followed her. They raced from the field towards the safety of the village. Most of them probably didn't even know what caused the explosion.

Marius stepped forward, his arms stretched towards to his torn-up field and missing flock. "But, my sheep!"

Magic, I've just seen magic, I thought. Far from the glorious, shining thing I'd read about and imagined all my life, it left a strange eerie feeling in my spirit, like slime on my soul.

Igor still stood with his chest puffed out. He looked about at the circle of remaining villagers—those who had not fled. He seemed to expect applause.

But Marius stared daggers at him.

Gus glowered as he wrenched himself up and dusted himself off. "What the fuck were you trying to do? Kill us?"

"What's the matter with you?" someone called from the dark.

"I can't hear!" someone cried. "My ears! I hear ringing!"

"You could've killed people," Arne, the cobbler, said, approaching Igor. His furious eyes settled on the open case, its contents a newly discovered danger. "What were you thinking?"

"He *did* kill my sheep!" Marius reminded us.

"The wolves will have fled deeper into the forest," Dag said, approaching. "They won't come back tonight."

Igor's face fell as the criticism surrounded him. His brow furrowed with confusion, and he deflated. It was almost comical, the transformation that overcame him. I realized he'd expected this display to turn everyone to his side, and it had worked out just the opposite. He was an injured child in a laughing crowd, nursing hurt pride that even his magical potions couldn't cure.

He looked away from them all, his face tilting down and towards me. And so I saw the transformation of his face from hurt and confusion into anger. Then he looked back up with yellow eyes full of hatred. They darted from person to person as he stored the memories of our faces. They settled on me last of all.

"That's fine," Igor said quietly. His voice sounded final, cold and false. He pressed his shoulders back and lifted his chin. "That's just fine. I'll find someone who *will* understand."

He left after that, snapping his case neatly closed and carrying it away with him.

Dag put a hand on Gus's shoulder. "You alright?"

"Of course," Gus said gruffly, though his finger kept going to his ear.

"What will I do now?" Marius wailed. "Half the hunt has gone back to the village, and I've lost more sheep than ever."

"I'm not going anywhere," Dag promised. "I can keep watch on the flock the rest of the night, and we can hunt another night. Or, we can take the hunt into the woods."

"I say we go into the woods," Gus said grimly. "The rest

of the pack must still be close. Without the deserters, it'll be easier. Most of them were worse than useless. We should take a small party out into the woods to track what's left of the pack."

Dag nodded.

"Let's do it," Arne said.

Marius expressed his gratitude as others volunteered to join the party.

But I slipped silently away. Following a strange urge, I tried not to run as I followed the apothecary's steps. His last words to me rang between my ears.

I'll find someone who will *understand.*

Aurora was back at the shop with Ulf. And I could not stop remembering how Igor had looked at her.

CHAPTER 7

THE DOOR TO our shop was open when I reached it. The bell lay on the floor with a crack in the lip. Inside, the shop was torn up. Sticks of smoked meat lay scattered as if a bad dog had had its way in here. Files and folders had spilled out from behind the counter to carpet the floor.

A seeping coldness started in my heart and crept through my body. An urgency filled me to know the location of every member of my family.

"Aurora," I called. "Ulf? Dad?" My feet carried me forward, and soon I was running, throwing myself around corners, eyes grasping to process what they saw as soon as I came anywhere new. There was nobody in the cellar or the back of the shop. I raced to the house and threw open the door.

The house was calm and untouched, every piece of furniture in its proper place. Ulf sat on a long bench, his huge form hunched over. He rocked back and forth, his muscles clenching and unclenching. I hadn't seen him like this since he was a boy who sat in the corner, clutching his arm and cowering when the neighbor's dog barked. Though I remembered this vividly, I'd been but a small child myself and unable to help.

I approached carefully, not wishing to startle him.

"Ulf. What happened?"

Ulf looked up at me. No tears had fallen, but his cheeks were ruddy from where he'd pressed his fists into them. His eyes were wide and lost. "She's gone."

Ice in my veins made me shiver. "Who?"

But who else could *she* be?

"Aurora. Aurora and Greta."

"Where did they go?"

"He came to the shop. That damned old apothecary who's been hanging around. I don't like the way he eyes her—I've said it from the beginning!" His eyes bulged as if he'd known this was coming, and if only we'd listened to him, perhaps she could've been saved.

I nodded. He had not yet surprised me. This was what I expected to find when I came here, I realized.

"What did he do, Ulf?"

"He—" Ulf shuddered. "I don't know! I don't know, Rune. It's like my memory isn't right." He squinted with the effort of remembering. "He said he'd come to marry her. 'Not on your life,' I said."

"What did Aurora do?"

"She was scared, Rune. She stepped behind me with Greta. And we figured, you know, that they'd be safe. What was the man going to do? Take them from me?" He huffed and flexed his huge muscles. It was hard to imagine the small-framed older man overcoming my powerfully-built brother. "I even grabbed a knife. Something about him was just that threatening. I had it *in* my hand."

"So what happened?"

Ulf stopped. His whole body froze and his eyes darted, searching through the past for answers. Then he shrugged. "I don't know. I don't know! They were gone, and the shop was a wreck. I don't remember if I tried to stop him. I don't remember why I couldn't." His scared eyes sought me out. "Rune, what's wrong with me?"

"I don't think there's anything wrong with you. Igor is a sorcerer. I just saw him do magic in Marius' fields. He must've used some kind of spell on you."

"A spell?" Ulf practically whined. "I don't believe in nonsense like that."

"Believe it or not." The evidence was stamped all over our shop and in Ulf's own mind.

Ulf stood up suddenly. He swayed on his feet before planting them firmly. He turned towards me and I breathed a sigh of relief. My brother was back, a look of determination and strength on his face. "We go take her back. Now."

I nodded, but my mind was flying like a bird amongst trees. Igor was powerful enough to get past Ulf. Ulf couldn't even remember how. If Ulf and I went after him on our own, how could we expect a different result?

"We need Dag and Gus and Father, too."

"What? But if we wait—"

"I know!" I cut in sharply. I knew what might happen to our sister if we waited. But what might happen to her if we failed to get her back tonight? That was worse—that was terrible—to even think about. I glanced behind me, out the door. "Gus and Dag are with the hunt. They're probably in the woods by now. Where's Father?"

Ulf's empty expression told me the answer. I sighed. "Get him. I'll run to the woods for the others. We meet back here, soon as we can."

Ulf nodded, determination hardening his face. For my entire childhood, I'd looked up at that face and felt safe. Nobody could come for me because Ulf would stand before them. Ulf would stop them. But he hadn't been able to help Aurora.

A worm of worry burrowed a tunnel through my chest. Worry that not even all of us together could help her now.

CHAPTER 8

I RAN TOWARDS Marius' fields.

The run had never felt so far. Had the road itself lengthened? At every strange sound in the trees, I flinched. The apothecary's laugh echoed between my ears. Was his magic at work here, or was it all in my mind?

I found myself at Cat's house and wondered why I'd slowed instead of continuing on to her father's fields and the woods on the other side of them. Then I knew why suddenly, a shocking discovery. My hand froze in the act of knocking. I lingered before her door. Then, not knowing why, I slipped around back and knocked on the shutters of her window instead.

She threw them open. Cat's brown hair was down, and wisps twisted beside her face. Her dancing eyes locked on me, and the excitement dimmed.

"I'm not my brother," I said in apology.

She recovered her smile. "What's up, Rune?"

I knew now why I'd stopped here, but still the words I

needed to speak felt heavy with gravity and consequences. "I need Aurora's red dye," I told Cat. "I don't know where she keeps it at the house, and I don't have time to search. I know she gave some to you."

She laughed. "Tired of waiting, are you? Going to dye your clothes yourself? I wouldn't, Rune. Dora says it can be hard to get the color even…"

My face was stone, unsmiling. She caught sight of it and her words drifted off into silence. The color drained from her cheeks.

"Oh," she said quietly. She stood with me then, weighing her choice. Would she give me the poison or deny me? We'd known each other since we were less than one year old. "Why do you need it?"

The words wavered and quivered as they came out. "The apothecary took Aurora against her will. Greta too. We're all going to get them back."

Cat's breath came heavy, angry, scared. She put her hand on mine, which rested on the sill. "I'll come with you."

"No. He's a magician, Cat. He did something to Ulf when he took Aurora. I haven't seen Ulf like that since he was a boy. I don't know what else Igor can do. I couldn't stand it if you got hurt."

"She's my friend, too. So are you. And Dag—" Dag was more than her friend.

"So help her." My quiet words had no tone. I held out my open palm and waited.

Cat took deep, heaving breaths. Her brow was furrowed. I realized in this moment I'd brought adulthood and consequence to her door, even as it was dropped on mine. She went from the window to a bag on the floor. She reached inside and took out a vial. With shaking hands, she held it out the window.

Our hands met as my fingers closed around it. She did not let go. "Rune, this is very dangerous. It's okay on your skin, but *don't* touch that skin to your lips."

I nodded. I already knew this. It was why I'd come.

But Cat did not let me take it yet. The potion was her hostage. "I'm coming too," she said again.

"No."

"I'm not asking." She let the potion go, but turned from the window and reached for her coat. She would grab her bow next and be standing beside me in moments.

"Cat—" It must've been the anguish in my voice that made her turn back. "Please, no. I can't—I can't risk—"

I did not know how to tell her why I could not have her there without saying that I loved her more than any friend should.

But she saw. As she had since we were children, she understood me without needing to hear the words. Her face took on a horrible expression of pity and guilt. She loved my brother.

"Okay, Rune," she whispered. "May luck be with you all. And be careful." Cat returned to the window and grasped my hand tightly one more time. Then, with darting glances into the woods, she closed the shutters.

I ran through the pasture and into the woods. I was silent as a mouse, so silent that the hunters, their ears pealed for the crunch of paws on leaf litter, did not even hear me.

"Dag," I said on approach.

My brother swore, half drawing back before he realized it

was me.

"You have to come. Now."

"Rune, where'd you get off to? Could you please keep it quiet?"

"You have to come. Now," I said again.

Dag peered at me curiously. "I'm the best shot here, and the best tracker. What—" He stopped. His eyes were bright white orbs, the only moon. He knew me as the childish one, caught up in minor concerns, but he saw in my face that this was not that. "What is it?"

"Igor has taken Aurora and Greta. Ulf tried to stop him and couldn't."

Dag was silent. He'd witnessed the apothecary's magic himself tonight. If Ulf couldn't stop him...

Dag shouldered his bow and began to run. "Come on," he called back to me. I soon lost sight of him as he wove swiftly between the trees.

"Gus," I called. I delivered the same message, and then he was running too, Ulf's axe in his fist.

We flew over tree roots, over the grasses of the field, and down the cobblestone road. My brothers swore at the mess in the shop. Our heartbeats raced as one as we flew towards the house where we'd find Ulf and Father, ready to go.

But only Ulf stood ready when we arrived. Our father was asleep in the bedroom, snoring loudly. Ulf's eyes were fire. His fingers were clenched into fists, the skin white and red. Gus tossed him his axe and Ulf caught it.

"Forget him," Ulf said of our father. "Let's go."

CHAPTER 9

ULF'S FIST POUNDED on the wooden door of the tower Igor had, only this morning, suggested he might buy. Ulf had come back to himself. His muscles bulged in a sleeveless tunic with suspender straps over the shoulders. His fingers clenched and unclenched on his axe. I was so used to seeing him with it, it looked to me only like an extension of his long arm. But he'd never drawn human blood with it before.

My pocket held Cat's vial of poison. Dag's bow hung over his shoulder. Gus's cleaver was a dark shadow in his hand. There was no moon to cast light on its surface.

The apothecary threw open the door. His smile was wide and entirely unsurprised. He'd been expecting us. "Come in, come in! You're right on time."

Light poured from the brightly lit room. Sparse shelving displayed tins and vials. *How did he set up shop so quickly?*

Igor's clothes, always garish, were now excessive. Gold lace adorned nearly every inch of a bright blue overcoat. His shirt, also gold, was cut low, revealing a chest covered with curls of hair and a large black tooth, which dangled from a cord around his neck. His breeches perfectly matched his overcoat, and I had no idea where he'd found a cobbler to commission matching boots. The brilliant blue color made him look paler than usual, and accented the wrinkles that were only starting to form around his yellow eyes.

I should've known when I saw his ears, I thought. *I should've known when I saw his eyes and his teeth.*

My brothers and I glanced at each other, each of us afraid and angry and confused. It was not the welcome we'd expected, which of course was none at all. We shuffled one at a time through his door, and it closed behind us as if a hand had firmly pushed it.

Aurora stood in the corner. She wore a white dress of delicate lace. A low neckline flattered her curves and made me feel sick. It fit her perfectly, like he'd made it to her measurements. Her blond locks were curled and draped about her shoulders like a waterfall. Her face held no expression at all. Blank, like she wasn't even there.

"My dear, your family has arrived!" The apothecary looked at Aurora and beamed. She did not even flinch.

Ulf cast me a look of horror that mirrored my own. Gus and Dag were white with rage.

Greta was not in the room.

"Look," Gus said, stepping forward, our leader. "I don't know what strange magics you possess. Frankly, I don't care." He rolled his shoulders, showing himself to be a man not interested in fanciful things like magic. He had a cleaver and strong arms, and those were the weapons he would use to answer any threat, magical or not. "We've come to take our sister back. Come on, Aurora," he said, and held out his hand.

Aurora didn't take it. She did not even seem to hear his words. She wavered on her feet, swaying like she could hardly balance.

"What have you done to her?" I asked.

"Oh, you know women get so many nerves on their wedding day. They're so excited! Behave hardly like themselves at all."

"This is not her wedding day," I said. My voice sounded strangled and strange in my ears.

"Damn right it's not," Gus growled.

"Ah," Igor said. He gritted his teeth and shuffled on his feet. "But I'm afraid it is. You've missed it."

My heart sank in my chest like a heavy stone plummeting.

Igor leapt towards us, hands outstretched. "I understand! You're upset! Such a big day, and we decided to elope. You see, she is so close to her family, but your father didn't approve of us. I'm sure now that it's done—"

"It's not done," Gus growled, stepping forward. Ulf was barely behind him. The metal of their weapons gleamed. "Nothing is done."

"But you see, it is!" Igor shouted triumphantly. "We are already bound." He clutched to his precious doll, our sister, with possessive arms around her shoulders. His eyes gleamed in pleasure, in victory. "You would not untie two lovers bound in eternal bliss, would you?"

He laughed, and clicked his tongue against the front of his teeth. "Bad boys, bad boys. So selfish." His ssss's hissed like angry snakes.

"Selfish?" I repeated, unbelieving.

He was a madman, raving words of nonsense. He paced away from her and back. "Selfish! Since the moment I set foot in this town, I've been ridiculed and made an outcast. The cruelty of small minds full of fear! Prejudice. It is simply prejudice! You do not wish for my love and me to be together because I am not a man like you."

"If you mean you are not a good man," Dag said coldly, "then we agree."

Igor laughed, that sharp, cutting sound. He gestured with a lazy hand. "You believe yourselves to be good men?" he sneered.

At the moment, we didn't look much like it. Ulf's eyes were storm clouds and his axe shivered in his hand. Gus leaned forward, ruddy cheeks red and inflamed with anger. Dag stood tight, his eyes cold.

"Good men or not, Aurora belongs with people of her choosing. She has not chosen you."

"Enough talk, Rune," Gus growled.

Dag nocked an arrow and drew back.

Igor's lips curled, exposing his teeth. Every one of them came to a sharp point. His eyes were locked on the arrow point. "Do you think to frighten me, boy?" He asked Dag. His voice was shivering crystal about to shatter.

"Let her go!" Ulf screamed. His face was red and spittle flew from his mouth. He was done talking. He swung his axe high above his head and brought it down. I steeled myself in that instant to watch Igor split in half like a hollowed-out tree.

But when the blade came down, Igor was no longer there. The axe stuck deep in the wood floor and Igor was behind my sister, squeezing his hands around her upper arms, making her his shield. Her face was still expressionless. Igor thrust Aurora forward as Ulf tore his axe from the wood and stumbled back, as if he were afraid his axe might move on its own to cut her.

"You think to frighten me?!" the apothecary shouted. He threw back his head and laughed.

I looked at Dag. Dag, who could shoot a squirrel through the eye at a hundred paces.

A war was being fought in Dag's eyes. A hunter, calm and capable, weighed the risks and the odds. His skills against Igor's erratic behavior. A detached coldness, entirely unlike I'd seen in Dag's warm eyes before this night, battled a shivering child full of terror.

His eyes slid over to meet those of his twin.

Gus gave a subtle nod and began to scream. A warrior's cry. Ulf raised his axe and rushed forward. Gus headed for Aurora, his arms outstretched to grab her. Dag waited with a hunter's patience for his shot. I alone stood useless.

The picture before me flickered and I blinked in confusion. Igor, who had been behind my sister, was now halfway across the room. Ulf stood over him like a giant cornering a rat. Gus had a hand around Aurora's arm. An arrow stuck out of the wall near her head, but I hadn't seen the shot or heard it land.

A small wail entered my ear. Greta. I cocked my ear to trace its direction, but it did not come again.

Aurora would not leave without Greta. She would never leave her daughter with this monster. Retrieving Greta was the most useful thing I could do.

The wail came again. I was ready for it this time as the picture before me blinked once more. Ulf had Igor trapped.

Igor held up his arms in defense of his face, but the axe was falling. No, it should've been falling but it was frozen, as if the moving world had solidified into a picture.

But the wail continued. It was coming from upstairs.

As soon as I thought this, I found myself at the base of the stairs. Fletching from multiple arrows decorated the closest wall. I lifted my foot onto the first stair.

The crying upstairs grew louder as I lifted a foot to the second step. But a roar behind me turned me back to see a scene of horror.

Aurora's hands shook on the handle of Gus's cleaver, which was buried in her gut. Blood spread over the surface of her white lace dress. Gus's hands pressed against the wound, but red flowed fast between his fingers.

"Aurora!" I screamed. I rushed towards her. My hands were before me, ready to help staunch the bleeding.

But I could not reach her. The space between us, which was only a few steps, stretched out into a long hall. The sound of my boots echoed as they pounded the wooden planks, but I went nowhere. Before me, Aurora grew pale. Her knees buckled. She fell into a pile on the floor.

Gus was roaring. He clutched at Aurora like a doll with cut strings.

"You didn't do anything," Igor said. I spun to see him.

He stood in a corner, utterly calm. At his feet, Ulf lay crumpled. His axe was buried in his back like it was a stump. The handle stood up tall. Igor tugged his jacket down, straightened his clothes.

My eyes were wet and my throat tasted of bile. I looked for Dag and found him. One of his own arrows protruded from his eye. From upstairs, Greta's wail came again.

"You didn't do anything," Igor repeated.

And then the image dissolved. I was standing back where was before I first heard Greta's cry. Gus was headed to Aurora, and Ulf was cornering Igor, and Dag was drawing his bow.

Upstairs, I heard a wail.

Impossible, was a thought in the back of my mind, but the visceral taste of iron and bile were in my mouth.

I ran. I tackled Gus and ripped his cleaver from his hand.

"Put your bow down!" I screamed to Dag, but the vision was frozen again, and he did not hear me.

I rushed towards Igor. I slipped past Ulf and raised Gus's cleaver. Igor caught my eye and smiled. Blue smoke puffed around him as I thrust down. When it cleared, Igor was gone. Greta was there in his place, her little belly a ruined mess. I'd stabbed so hard, the cleaver stuck into the wood floor beneath her. I fell to my knees and dropped the knife.

A wail. Aurora coming to cradle her daughter, her voice a screech of agony that shuddered through me, raising goosebumps.

"Aurora," I said, my voice thick, "I didn't mean to."

Igor's laugh sounded in the air, pealing like a bell from every direction. I blinked and the picture changed. Aurora lay beside her bloody daughter now, the cleaver in her stomach. A circle of red spread through the white lace of Aurora's wedding dress.

I sat back on my heels. Tears dropped off my chin. I heard myself blubbering like a baby. I did not look around the room to see my brothers, for I knew what I'd find. I closed my eyes.

When I opened them, the vision had reset. A wail came from upstairs.

It was not real. I knew that now, and yet the heart-rending sights it showed me could not be unseen. I felt ripped raw and utterly uncertain.

"Gus!" I cried out. "Can you hear me, Gus?" I spoke not to the man in my vision, who was not real, but to the real Gus, who I suspected still stood just beside me. "Ulf! Dag!"

I listened, but all I heard were the screams of the phantoms in my vision.

The cry came again from upstairs. It seemed to center my entire vision, and so I followed it. I left the violence behind and climbed the stairs.

Each creaking step was a horror. Real or unreal, I did not wish to watch Greta die again, and I feared that merely by climbing the stairs, I might set that into motion.

I found her in a cradle by a bed. Candles were lit on side tables, and red wine sat untouched in goblets beside them. Greta wore white like her mother. She looked unharmed. Her face was puffed up red from crying.

I held no weapons except the poison that was still in my pocket. I reached into the cradle and lifted the baby up. I cradled her in my arms and rocked her until she quieted. I did not know if she was real. I did not know anymore if I was.

"No matter what I do, I do the wrong thing," I confided in her, and then I frowned. My fingers were wet. I held the baby away from me, and she was limp in my hands. The area around her mouth was stained red. Red dripped off her chin and down the front of her dress.

"She always was an untidy eater," Igor said behind me, as

if he'd known Greta for all the time she'd been alive.

"It's not real, it's not real, it's not real," I said as I placed the child back down gently in her cradle. My hands quaked. One of them held a glass vial, unstoppered and empty.

Igor laughed again. I turned to see him, though tears leaked down my face and dripped from my chin onto the floor, and my vision was hazy. His face was bright and cheery, utterly delighted. "Ah, but it could be. It's all your choice."

I was back downstairs.

Gus and Dag and Ulf were back with me in their starting places, and I thought the vision would begin again. I sniffled and wiped my eyes, hardening my heart for another round.

But Gus shuddered and lowered his cleaver. "What the fuck?" he said shakily.

Beside me, Dag was dropping his bow. His face was very pale.

From upstairs, there came the sound of a wail. My blood beat like the current of a cold river. I was frozen to the spot, terrified to move, terrified to make any choice lest it be wrong.

The apothecary was still behind my sister. His hands came off her arms and closed over her chest, like a hug, or a man drowning. Clenched between his finger and thumb, he held the black tooth from his necklace. He studied us all, his eyes serious and sad. And yet behind these falsehoods, almost hiding but not quite, was glee.

"I see that you all will not wish us a happy marriage." He sighed with great drama. "That's a shame. I'd hoped to welcome you into my home tonight and feast with you and accept your gifts with gratitude."

There was no feast laid on the table, and the gifts we

carried were steel and poison.

"But I see now that no such happy future will occur." He let go of my sister and came around her. Stepping forward, a big deliberate step, rolling from his flamboyant yellow boot heel to his toe. His eyes settled on each of us in turn. Ulf first, and then Gus, then Dag, and finally, me. I could read no expression in them but intense concentration. I was rooted to the spot as he bored into me, and I could not look away.

His finger rubbed the tooth's jagged, black edge. A single red drop rolled down it and splattered on the wooden plank.

"No, no happy future for you or yours, you who feared instead of loved. For this sin I curse you, from this day until the end of time, to be haunted by your own fear. For whatever you fear most, you will become. And there will be no escape."

The sorcerer's voice vibrated with conviction. Another blood droplet fell from his pierced finger. Two more.

And then we were outside. The night was dark, the sky moonless. Ulf breathed heavily, as if he'd been running. Gus was still shaking, and Dag was so pale he was practically translucent in the night.

"What do we do now?" Ulf asked. He looked first to Gus, but Gus had no answer. So he looked to Dag.

Dag shouldered his bow. He moved slowly, his muscles stiff or tired. "We go home."

"We can't go home!" Gus exclaimed. "We have to *do* something!"

Dag nodded. "Yes, of course, but first we go home."

He walked away and the rest of us followed. Behind us, I heard a wail from the tower's upstairs window. It haunted me, ringing in my ears.

CHAPTER 10

WE GATHERED ALL together in our home. But we weren't all together. Aurora and Greta weren't there. We stood silent and still, each of us horrified by his own inaction, each of us unsure what to do next.

"We can gather the whole village," Gus said. "Get every man with a pitchfork over there right now. He can't stop them all."

I looked despairingly at my older brother, but Dag said it first. "Of course he can stop them all."

Dag was still so pale. He leaned against a table like a weakened animal that had only just managed to escape a trap. He stumbled to a cabinet and retrieved a bottle of our father's spirits. He threw it back and wiped his mouth, stoppered the bottle, and threw it to Gus. Gus looked at his twin strangely and put the bottle down.

I searched my memories of the tales I'd read of sorcery. Of the rumors and whispers brought to town on market day. "They say there's a witch in Sleepy Bramsville. Maybe she..."

"You want to leave our sister alone with that monster for a week? Leave town to go chase some story of a witch?" Dag scoffed. "That does sound like one of *your* ideas, Rune."

I'd never heard him speak like this, but he was right. My ideas were always awful. Look at what happened in that tower. Every choice I made was wrong.

"We have to do something!" Gus said again, as if we were arguing against it.

"Of course we do." Dag spat the words. He began to pace the tight room like a caged animal, his brow furrowed, his face not like his own at all. His hand clenched and unclenched on his bow, which he had not put down when we came into the house.

"Hey, what did you guys see when we were over there?" I asked. My mind was spinning, deciphering the experience. I sought the cracks in Igor's magic, if there were any.

"What are you talking about?" Gus asked.

"I-I saw things that weren't real." I didn't want to say what. Was I the only one of us who had the visions?

Dag stilled, but without calm. Like a predator crouched in grass. "I saw things. I…did things. But they weren't real." He shuddered and went for the bottle at Gus's feet to take another swig.

Gus nodded. "I kept trying to rescue Aurora, but no matter what I did, I couldn't reach her. It kept resetting, and each time I'd try again. But I was chained, or I was far away, or a whole army of people was between us. No matter what, I couldn't get to her."

"I saw none of those things," I said, "but I had visions of my own."

"Ulf?" Gus turned to our brother. Ulf sat quietly on a bench. He'd said nothing since we left the tower. Now we all turned to him.

"I don't feel well," he said thickly. He held his head in sweating palms. As I watched, he slumped and slid forward.

"Catch him," I said. I leapt forward, but Dag was closest. He managed to intercept my brother's fall, though he was so much smaller than Ulf, he simply acted as a cushion as Ulf crashed to the floor. I knelt on one side, with Gus on the other.

Ulf's eyes were closed. His lids fluttered and a sweat had broken out across his forehead, which was red and hot. The scars from his childhood trauma stood out extra white on his arms, and his red hairs were raised in goosebumps across his body.

"What is this? What's wrong with him?" Gus asked.

"The sorcerer cursed him," Dag said. "Didn't you hear him? He cursed us all."

For this sin I curse you, from this day until the end of time, to be haunted by your own fear. For whatever you fear most, you will become. And there will be no escape.

I placed a hand on my own forehead. Did I feel hot too? It was hard to tell when rage and terror and sadness still roiled inside me like a ship caught in a storm. I did feel too hot; I did feel shaky. But it was only from the thought of my sister caught in that sick man's trap. I was pretty sure.

"Curses aren't real," Gus said, but he didn't sound certain.

"Oh yeah, then what's wrong with him?" Dag's voice held an edge. His eyes were cutting as he glared, and…

I grabbed my brother's face and twisted it towards me.

"Hey!" said Dag, tearing himself out of my grip. "What

are you doing?"

"Look at me. It could be the firelight."

"What could be the firelight?" Dag stilled and allowed me to twist his head. My tone was too urgent. Our heartbeats were the only sound as I stared.

"Your eyes. I think they're changing color."

Dag scoffed and pulled out of my grip. "Don't be stupid." He bent over Ulf, who'd begun shuddering. "We have to help him."

"I don't know how," Gus admitted. The anguish was clear in his voice.

My brain was a bird in flight, but it only fluttered about, settling nowhere. Afraid to choose wrong.

Ulf began to seize. His giant body convulsed, his shins slamming against a table leg until Dag kicked it violently out of the way.

Gus held Ulf's head on his lap, trying to keep him steady. "What the fuck is happening?" he whispered.

My throat was so dry, I could not speak. I didn't know what to do.

Then Ulf began to grow. It was subtle at first. I thought it was only his writhing that brought him closer to me. I slid back, but his shaking fingertips soon reached me again.

"I think—" I started.

Then his back cracked and twisted.

Gus roared in horror and Dag went silent, his eyes wide. Ulf's back cracked again and he screamed, rage and agony in his voice. He flailed his arms, grasping for something to hold onto. I reached for his hand to hold it. But his fingers became claws, long, curved, and black. The hair on his body grew longer and darkened. It sprouted up over every inch of his body. His legs cracked like his back and grew in a new direction. His clothes were shredded.

But it wasn't until his face began to change that I knew.

The black tooth in Igor's hand. Four droplets of blood.

For whatever you fear most, you will become.

"Get back. Back!" I cried. I ran to Gus, who still held Ulf's head as Ulf's nose lengthened into a snout with a wet black nose. I tugged Gus away. The twins and I stumbled against the far wall.

But Ulf was not done growing. The wooden table shattered as a tail grew from him and whipped against it. The bench was thrust against the back wall. It creaked at the strain of the pressure.

"What's happening?" Dag asked.

"He's becoming a wolf."

But Ulf was not just a wolf. He was a wolf larger than a horse. He grew until I feared he would outgrow our living room. His body pressed us against the walls, trapping us. Would he even have room to stand?

His seizing slowed and stopped. Ulf the wolf lay sprawled in a strange shape on the floor. He was shaking and weak. He whined, a high keening sound. He twisted and tried to stand.

His legs were unsteady under him. He was not used to having four of them, but he mastered them and stood up, his tail waving as he sought balance.

His head grazed the vaulted ceiling.

"Ulf," I said uncertainly.

Ulf's head whipped to look at me. His eyes were as yellow as the sorcerer's. His ears were pointed and his teeth, when he growled at us, were weapons of death.

I stepped forward, though I could not go far, and held up my hands in a gesture of peace. My heart raced in my chest. I did not know if my brother was still in there.

The wolf regarded me without movement. I could see nothing of what he was thinking, if he was thinking at all. Then his gaze turned towards the small door that was the only exit.

His muscles bunched.

"Get back!" I shouted, shoving my brothers into the bedroom. The wolf ran at cottage wall, ducking his head. He smashed through the logs like they were nothing. He darted into the street as wood creaked and timber fell. Gus threw himself over our father's passed-out body as the roof collapsed.

When the sky stopped falling, dust and wood shavings filled the air. Nails poked out of fallen boards, and logs made a maze.

"Did you see which way he went?" I coughed.

Dag pointed down the road that led to Marius' farm.

My blood was cold. "He's headed for Cat's."

Dag coughed and wiped dust off his shoulder. He inspected his bow. "He'll just pass her and go into the woods."

I stared at him like he was someone I didn't know. "You can't know that. He's dangerous right now! Look what he did!"

"He was just trying to get out," Gus said, like he was trying to convince himself.

"Maybe, maybe not," I said.

Gus swore.

"What is it?"

"The hunting party is still out in the woods."

"So? They can't kill *him*." Dag spoke of our brother as if

he were a monster, a horrifying monster with boils on his face and evil in his heart.

"No, but he could kill them," I said.

"He's Ulf. He'd never—" Gus started.

"He might," Dag cut in. "If he's not himself."

"We don't know what this is," I said. "We don't know if it's changed more than just his body." I looked around helplessly at the torn-up house. "He did this. Was he in pain? Was he afraid? Or was he caught in some animal rage? We can't know. And until we do, we can't let him come upon that hunting party."

Dag nodded. His neck was stiff and his face was cold. "We go after him."

Gus's brow was furrowed, his eyes lined with worry. He looked empty-handed and helpless, standing there with his big muscles and nothing to use them for. Carefully, he navigated the wreckage to retrieve his cleaver.

"Let's go," he said quietly, "before he gets too far ahead."

CHAPTER 11

THE HUNT WAS still out.

This was the only thought that went through my head. It spun around like a child circling a tree trunk, wild, about to slip, as we followed Ulf's path towards the woods. It was not hard to follow his trail. Trees lined the narrow streets of Baneswood and their lowermost branches were broken.

"This way," Dag pointed above our heads, but we did not need his skills. Fallen branches littered the path. It was eerily quiet. No sprites flitted between the trees. Even the scratching of the night forest's creatures seemed to have ceased, as if they all hid from the monster.

My heart pounded until the houses thinned out and we passed Cat's. It seemed Ulf had fled into the woods.

But the hunt. The hunt was still out.

We flew into Marius' fields. The sheep were asleep—a good sign—until we plowed into their midst and they woke, bleating protestations.

"What is it, Rune? You spot something?" a villager cried

out. Some of them must've stayed behind as guards when the hunting party went out. I couldn't tell whose voice spoke over the beating of my own heart, but her shadow raced towards us and began to follow. I cast my gaze back and saw others.

Shit.

We would lead the hunt right to Ulf. I slowed and stopped, signaling my brothers to stop too.

"We can't," I said quietly. "We'll just lead them to him and make it worse."

But just then, off to my right, a scream.

"Too late," Gus said.

We ran.

Dangling pine branches slapped my face as I dodged through the trees, jumping roots I'd navigated for years. Dag kept pace while Gus, not knowing the land quite as well, lagged behind.

I saw Ulf first, a towering blackness. He reared up like a man, like he didn't know how to stand on four legs. His head was in the branches. They broke off and fell like shrapnel around the forces of the village, who pressed at him with their pitchforks.

Ulf backed away and did not attack. He roared his fear. A strange and strangled scream issued from his giant snout.

Though they held their weapons high to keep him back, the villagers did not attack either. This magical abomination was far more dangerous than the wolves they'd expected to find on their hunt tonight.

But the slightest shift could tip the scales.

"Stop!" I cried. "Everybody stop!"

My neighbors whirled on me, weapons raised. Their heads

whipped back and forth between me and the menace. I raised my empty hands.

"All of you, stop. That is not a wolf, and it's not a monster. It is my brother Ulf. The apothecary cursed him, and—"

Ulf backed away on two legs as I spoke. He collided with the blacksmith's apprentice, who'd frozen to hear my words. Ulf wobbled and fell onto four legs. The young man stabbed out in fear of being crushed, and his spear grazed Ulf's belly.

Ulf whined. His eyes were wide and white and afraid.

"He's cornered!" someone shouted. "Get him!"

Emboldened by the voice, the apprentice, Ivan, thrust out his pitchfork towards Ulf's face. Ulf's eyes grew round as the fork points came close. He growled, his hairy forehead creased above yellow eyes. His huge teeth bared.

"Again!" someone shouted, even as I shouted, "No!"

The pitchfork snapped out again, and the young man, stupid and brave, stepped closer along with it. Ulf's teeth snapped a warning near the man's face. With a sinking feeling, I felt us to be on a cart running wildly away down a steep hill, and all it would take was a single pebble to overturn us.

"Ulf!" I cried. "Ulf, no!"

Ivan was spooked by Ulf's snapping teeth and fell back, but others jumped to his aid. I could not get to my brother through the crowd of them. They surrounded Ulf, his tail against the trunk of an ancient oak, and held out the points of their weapons.

He snapped out at their circle, monstrous teeth closing over and over on air. He was only trying to scare them back, not hurt them.

But they did not see his restraint. They saw only snapping

teeth. They advanced.

Ulf circled around the tree and stumbled back, back. And when he tripped they ran at him, and he snapped out one more time...

"Ulf!" Gus and Dag and I cried his name as the blades came down.

Ulf's teeth closed on the cobbler Arne's arm. The white spear points of his teeth punctured deep, and the man screamed, a sound of agony that drove the birds from the trees. Ulf shook his head like a dog with a bone, and thick red blood leaked from the punctures.

Ulf's own arm came to me like a vision. I'd seen the scars a thousand times. White and thick and rough to touch. Ulf let go and Arne's heart pumped his blood onto the forest floor.

The villagers stumbled back, weapons falling from hands. They began to run away.

"You idiots, come back!" Gus screamed. "Somebody wrap the wound!" His face was white and his eyes were orbs of panic.

Gus rushed forward to pull the cobbler back. The blacksmith pulled off his shirt to use as a bandage, and a belt became a tourniquet. But poor Arne's face was already so pale.

"I heard that new apothecary say he had healing potions," someone said. "We have to get Arne to him. It's his only hope."

"No!" I wanted to shout, but the word stuck in my throat because they were right, of course. I wondered if he'd planned it this way.

But even as a few dragged the cobbler away, those left were not done with Ulf. The strongest of them, those with axes and muscles and eagerness to prove themselves, pressed him back. He growled at them, snapping his jaws, but he did not attack again. His eyes darted to Arne, misery in their depths. He licked blood off his teeth.

"Ulf, run," I begged.

The village carpenter lunged, her axe swinging, anger in her roar. Ulf batted her aside. The woman hit a trunk and went down hard, and the others pressed in one after the other. They were no longer hesitant, no longer waiting and timid and afraid. They swung their weapons like wild fiends, over their heads and across their bodies. I wondered that they did not hit each other instead of him.

"No!" Gus ran forward and shoved one of the men from behind.

Dag was right behind him. He punched a man in the face, but the man was much bigger than him and hit back. Dag's bow skittered away, and they wrestled on the ground.

"Go, Ulf, go!" I shouted again. This could only get worse so long as he was here. "Go deep in the woods. We'll find you!"

The wolf's eyes locked on mine, then moved to my brothers. We fought for him against men and women we'd known since birth. Ulf took a step back, and then another, and finally darted into the woods. He disappeared faster than the mob could follow.

"Come on," I said. The group dragging the cobbler had not gotten far. "Gus, Dag, come and help. We have to get Arne back to the village." If Arne died, it would make my brother a murderer, and this I could not fathom, not in the most speculative parts of my brain. Not Ulf. Not ever.

Gus rushed towards the party, but Dag stood over the

body of the man he'd knocked unconscious. His chest was heaving, and his fist was bloodied and still clenched. He looked up at me, chin tucked like a man in a boxing ring. "I'm not going back there," he said.

"What?!"

Gus was trying to help lift the cobbler up. The heels of Arne's boots dragged along the forest floor, catching fallen needles and furrowing tracks. But the party shoved Gus away when he reached them, their angry faces turned on him.

"The fuck are you protecting a monster for?"

"It's your fault Arne's going to die!"

"What? No!" Gus followed them helplessly, hands raised. "The wolf is Ulf! He didn't want to hurt anybody! Didn't you see him holding back?"

"Holding back?!" they replied.

Arne's face was white and his head lolled weakly. He'd passed out and was just dead weight, but the villagers wouldn't let Gus help them lift.

"Fuck them," Dag spat as he watched the slow procession. "You see them Rune, same as me. They don't want us back and I'm not begging. What's hard about that to understand? I'm going after Ulf. I'll keep watch over him in case they come back."

I was flummoxed. Ulf could take care of himself. The village was our home. Being there was the best way to know if they were sending out another hunt.

"We should all stick together," I said.

"Stick together?" My brother advanced towards me, and for a sudden cold moment I felt afraid. Then I remembered that this was Dag, the kindest man I knew. "Rune, we're not *together*. Aurora is trapped in the home of that *freak* right now!" His eyes bulged as he considered what might be happening to her. I could see the agony of his imaginings in his face, which looked sick and enraged at once. As for me, I couldn't think about it. "And Ulf is that thing—" he pointed into the woods where our brother had run "—that the people we grew up with just tried to stab to death! So no matter which way you go, Rune, we're not together. You choose your way."

With that, Dag turned from me and loped into the woods after Ulf. I stood for a moment, totally alone, and then I turned silently and followed the blood trail leaking from the cobbler. I'd find Gus and Father back in the village. We'd figure out what to do.

CHAPTER 12

I WENT BACK into the village but I did not know what to do next. Gus dropped away from the villagers as they carried the cobbler to Igor's and knocked upon his door. Gus told me Igor opened it still wearing his gold and blue suit, and Gus thought of pushing in to seize Aurora but didn't. For if Arne died, it would be Ulf who had killed him. And so the apothecary must live, for now.

The Gus who returned home after that was defeated. Blood soaked a once-white shirt. I'd seen blood on my brother, the butcher, for many years, but this was different. Redder for being human. He dropped heavily on the bench that Ulf had sat upon before he turned.

Our father was still asleep in his room. I wondered if he'd woken to notice the destruction of our home. Perhaps he thought he'd done it himself in a drunken haze.

Gus buried his head in his hands. "I can't think anymore, Rune," he said. "I'm not smart. I don't know what to do."

"I don't know what to do either," I admitted.

"Yes, but I'm supposed to know what to do," Gus spat. "It feels just like in his house, in that trick world he showed us. I kept seeing him about to kill Aurora. Right behind her was an open door, and she could've run, but of course she ran towards Greta instead. I had my cleaver in my hand. I was standing right there. So close, Rune. So close I could've cut down Igor with a swing of my arm.

"But I couldn't move at all. And then *that damned boy*—" and I knew, for I knew Gus, that he meant Otto, Greta's father "—was there, and he shoved me out of the house. I couldn't open the door; I couldn't get back to them. Then, like a loop, it all started again. Every time, the same. Sometimes an army between her and I. Sometimes *that boy* took her away. Sometimes nothing; I just couldn't move.

"No matter what, I couldn't do anything to get her back, Rune. No matter what I did, I couldn't help. What did you see?"

Something bloodier, and full of choices that were really traps. Why show us different things? Unless...

"You were helpless," I said quietly.

Gus bristled, as if even the suggestion that he might be helpless in a strange and magical vision was insulting. "What are you saying?"

"That's your worst fear. Has been since the day that wolf got Ulf."

Gus's body was stiff with remembering. "So?"

"Ulf's greatest fear is wolves."

Now Gus stilled. His face, his eyes, became very afraid. "What are you saying?" he asked more quietly.

"Igor cursed us. What was it he said? 'For this sin I curse

you, from this day until the end of time, to be haunted by your own fear. For whatever you fear most, you will become.' And now Ulf is a wolf. And you're sitting here and you don't know what to do."

Again, Gus bristled. He wanted to deny it, but it was true. "So? What about you? What about Dag?"

I tried to think of what I feared most, but it isn't always as easy to see yourself. "I don't know. I don't know. I'm still figuring it out." I began to pace. "Ulf became a wolf almost as soon as the curse was cast, as if that was the easiest fear for the curse to dig its teeth into."

"And what about the rest of us? You think we're all going to change into something?"

"I don't know," I said again. "We might change too. That's all I can say. I think we might."

Gus stood suddenly. "Well I'm not going to sit here and wait for some…some *curse* to come for me." He puffed up his muscles. "If it wants me, it can come and find me and take me."

He headed for the room where our father slept. He flipped the man over, and our father fell off the bed onto the floor. The thud woke him and he swore.

"Come on, old man. We need you, and it's damn time you showed up."

Gus left our father blinking in confusion on the floor and rubbing his ass. Gus marched around the living room righting furniture. Then he headed for the door and out onto the street.

I ran after him. Blearily, our father followed.

"Where are you going?" I shouted.

"I'm going to assemble a goddamn army. We're going to

throw this guy out of our village and get Aurora back." Gus stopped at our nearest neighbor's and pounded hard on the wooden door. It was before dawn. If they weren't a part of the hunt, they were probably deep in sleep.

"You can't go back there." I grasped tight to my much bigger brother's arm and tried to tug him from the door. He slipped easily from my grasp.

"Our sister is back there," he roared, pointing towards the tower where Igor held her imprisoned. "I can't *not* go back." He looked at me, disgusted. "Honestly, Rune, what's the matter with you?"

I took a deep breath in and let it out slowly. Shame crept through me. Yes, I felt like a disgusting, shameful animal for not advocating that we march over there right now, weapons drawn, and do anything—*anything*—to get her back. But we'd already tried. Four of us. And now there were only two. "You have no reason to think it'll go any differently than last time. We need a new plan. We have to try something different."

"I am trying something different. I am going to bring every goddamn person in this town with me. Let's see him enchant them all."

Someone opened the door. In rushed tones, Gus explained. He begged for their help. His voice was anguished, that of a father. Although he was Aurora's brother, he'd always acted like more. He'd taken over in Father's shop and taken over his duties as parent, too. He'd spent his whole life doing everything he could for all of us. Now he could do nothing.

I couldn't get the thought out of my head. It hung over me like a blade that might fall at any moment.

I split from him and went door to door. I greeted each

answering neighbor by name. I reminded them, with a warm question or two, that we'd known each other all our lives. I cared about them, as they surely did me. And then I asked them to come and help save my sister. Their eyes darkened as I told the tale.

A magician, I said, with an evil heart. He'd kidnapped my sister and married her against her will. He'd cursed our brother and he might do worse to others if we did not banish him now. Their faces clouded over. They reached for their weapons, or their tableware, and they agreed: They'd never liked him. Something about him, it was just something about him.

I arrived at the apothecary's tower with an entourage in tow. Gus was already there, shifting impatiently from foot to foot, his cleaver in hand. Behind him ranged villagers with alarmed faces. They looked like he had dragged them from their houses, like he'd given them no choice but to follow him here at the crack of dawn.

"Finally," Gus said, and he kicked open the door.

"Be careful," I warned everyone. "Igor's powerful and dangerous."

Our army rushed inside.

The apothecary sat in a rocking chair with a pipe. Beside him in another rocker sat my sister. My heart broke at the still-blank look on her face, but she was clean and visibly unharmed. She wore a light blue dress which fell lightly about her as she stitched a pattern that said "Home sweet home."

Gus rushed to her and grabbed her. He tore her up from her rocker and she cried out from the pain of his hand on her arm.

"Gus! What are you doing?" She struggled against him. In

shock, he loosened his grip and she ripped herself free. She glared up at him and threw down her needlework. There was something subtle in the expression of her face that looked nothing like her at all, but if you hadn't grown up alongside her then you wouldn't know it.

"Come on, Aurora. Get behind me." Gus held his cleaver up as if to cut the apothecary down the moment he stood. But the apothecary did not stand. He only sat and smiled at the fire that crackled in his small hearth. He allowed his wife to speak for him, let her vitriol pollute the righteous anger of the crowd.

"Gus, you get out of here right now. You have no right to barge into my home and try to take me from my rightful husband, just because you don't like him. Truly, this is bullying of another level." She cast her gaze to the crowd, and when I looked closely, I saw her mouth moved in strange ways, as if she were trying to form words that were not those she spoke. A little spit dribbled from the corner of her lips, and she did not wipe it away. "You," she called to the baker's wife. "Did you come here of your own volition, or did Gus bully you too?"

The baker's wife shifted from foot to foot, looking down.

A sinking weight in my chest suggested to me where this was going. I felt hot and then suddenly cold.

"And you—why are you here? Do you not remember Arne, who was saved by my husband only hours ago? Are your memories so short? Your prejudices so strong?"

The crowd stilled. Shame permeated the room. They'd come to exile this man for his strangeness, and now they were abashed.

"He *has* helped us," a woman murmured. The crowd

seemed to agree.

The corner of the apothecary's lip twitched up just slightly. He tried not to let it show. In his fingers, he held his blackened wolf's tooth. He passed it from one finger to the next, caressing its sharp edge.

I begged the crowd to see through his tricks. "He has used magic to bewitch my sister. She did not wish to marry him. She told me herself. Please, just help us take her from him, and you will see."

"Maybe she was just afraid to tell you the truth," the baker suggested, eying the towering form of my brother. "It's not unheard of for a young lady to elope with a man her father disapproves of."

"That's not what's going on!" Gus screamed. His face was bright red, and he tried to grab Aurora's arm again. He would drag her from this place if he had to do it alone. But the men of the village pulled him off her, pulled him back.

Breathing heavy, the baker asked her, "Are you happy in your marriage?"

Aurora nodded. An expression of bliss came over her face, like a woman who has already drowned and now floats in the water, utterly at peace.

The plan was crumbling. My sister was enchanted, my brother was held in strong hands by village men who considered him a bully, and Igor sat at ease in his rocker with the smallest smile on his face.

In my pocket I still carried Cat's vial of poison. I cast my gaze about, looking for any way I might use it. I could rush the apothecary, unstoppering the vial and spilling it on his face. But my sister stood protectively over his chair. It was too risky.

As I considered, Gus acted. A sickening crack sounded as he thrust his elbow into the baker's face. The man crumbled, holding his nose, and my brother shrugged off the grip of his other jailer.

A chuckle started in the rocker by the fire as my brother raised his cleaver high in the air. Gus's eyes were fire and his skin was fire and I jumped forward to shove Aurora out of the way, lest she try to put herself between Gus and his target.

But Gus never finished his lunge. Instead, he stumbled. His cleaver fell from his hand and he croaked, grabbing at his throat. His hand was malformed. He scratched his own throat, then held his hands forward in horror as he watched his fingers become claws. Hair sprouted across their surface and then his arms lengthened, becoming legs.

Igor laughed and laughed as Gus fell forward, heaving in agony. "You seem to have a wolf problem in this town," Igor said.

Men backed away, fright painting their faces. My heart sank, horror filling every crevasse of my chest as Gus became a wolf so big, he was trapped inside the house.

The villagers were torn between the door and the pitchforks in their hands. Should they run or should they fight? Some of them had encountered Ulf and did not wish to fight another wolf of his size.

"Help, help!" screamed Aurora, her mouth working strangely. One eye watched me, and the other stared straight ahead.

"Kill it!" a voice shouted. "Kill it before it hurts my daughter!"

Stunned, I turned and stared in cold horror at my father,

who seemed to have somehow forgotten that the creature was his own son.

That decided them. The men ran forward, battle cries loud, and tried to kill the man who sold them the meat for their tables.

"Stop!" I screamed. "It's Gus! It's a trick! It's a curse! Stop!"

Gus was only now getting shakily to his feet. I rushed to block the villagers who charged him, but I was small, and they threw me aside.

The baker's wife spit down at me as I lay on the floor. Hatred deformed her face. How quickly it could rise up to consume a heart. "Your family is the curse. No wonder she wanted to get away from you! Get out of here and never come back!"

I lay on the floor, shock holding me like a boot on my chest.

I had to get Gus out of here, but he was cornered. The villagers backed him closer and closer towards the rocker where Igor still sat with a smile on his face.

But as Gus edged towards him, a new expression came into Igor's face. Was it concern? His eyes darted more and more often towards Gus, and he rose from his chair with what looked like deliberate calm. He walked at a stately pace towards the stairs, his eyes never leaving the monster who was getting very close.

"Gus!" I shouted. "He's trying to leave! Get him! Get Aurora!"

Igor's eyes flew to me and narrowed. In the next moment, the villagers rushed to stand between Gus and Igor. Aurora dodged around them all to join Igor at the base of the stairs. She took his hand.

Gus growled. He snapped at them, and Igor jumped. The villagers pressed against Gus with their staffs and forks and axes. He was panting and bleeding from half a dozen small wounds.

"Just get out!" I shouted. "Get out!"

And so Gus did the only thing he could do. He turned from Igor and Aurora and ran towards the door. Our father stabbed at him as he passed, grazing his side with a butcher's knife.

But Gus got stuck in the doorway.

Igor's laugh came again. "You can't help her now," he called, gleeful and confident once more.

I ran at my brother and threw all my weight at his tail. His body slipped a few inches further through the door, and I backed up to do it again. The crowd of villagers rushed me. I felt the sharp sting of a wound carve across my back, and something deep thudded against my arm, reverberating through me as I screamed and ran, ran as fast as I could at my trapped brother. I collided with him, and his body slid out the door. I tumbled after him. We collapsed together on the street outside the apothecary's tower.

As fast as we could, we bolted for the woods.

CHAPTER 13

OUR NEIGHBORS FOLLOWED after us with pitchforks and torches and hate. Axes gleamed on their shoulders and knives hung from their belts. My back burned, heat carving a line, and I itched where blood trickled down my skin.

Past Cat's house we ran. Past the place where Ulf had encountered the hunt last night. The sun rose and made everything look different, sparkling and bright. It wasn't hard to see the broken branches where Ulf had gone. We followed the path.

We found Dag first. An arrow was on his bow. He had us within his sights before I even made out his face, but he saw it was us and dropped his arm.

"Shit," he said, looking up at Gus, who panted heavily. Blood trickled from his many small injuries, and his chest heaved. "Oh, shit."

I couldn't name the expression that came into Dag's face at the sight of his twin. First stricken and shocked, and then it hardened. "It's going to happen to all of us," he said. "No way around it."

Ulf came into sight. He sniffed at Gus, nosing his injuries. He whined, and Gus made an answering sound. I wondered if they could understand each other.

"The village is on our tail. Gus changed in front of everyone. There's another hunt coming. We've got to go. We've all got to keep running, right now."

"We're not running anymore," Dag said. He twirled an arrow in his fingers. The metal edge of the tip caught the sunlight as it spun. There was an aloofness in him that had never been there before, like all his warmth had dried up in a drought.

Ulf sighed and laid down.

"What's the matter with him? Is he hurt?"

Dag shrugged. "No. Just lazy, I guess."

"Lazy?" That didn't sound like Ulf at all.

"Yeah. This morning some hunters setting traps were going to stumble across us. I was ready to fight them, but Ulf just lay down and stayed quiet, and they didn't see us."

I looked over at Ulf. "Maybe he's still in there."

"What?" Dag asked. His words were clipped and short, as if he didn't have time for them.

"Ulf. Maybe he's still in there. He was scared when he turned, right? Scared and confused. He was under attack. But now he seems more like himself. He didn't want to attack the hunters, so he hid to avoid confrontation. Ulf would never *want* to hurt anyone."

"Well, he doesn't have a choice now, does he?" Dag peered behind me, as if any minute the hunters might materialize between the trees.

I couldn't help but look too. They'd been so close behind us. They must've slowed, creeping forward, afraid to run too fast into danger.

Ulf growled. We looked at him, and he shook his head "no" very clearly, like a man.

I could've screamed and shouted, fist pumping in joy. "Yes! See? He's in there!"

Gus nodded. He was himself too, trapped in a monster's body.

But Dag looked dourly at Ulf. "What do you mean, 'no'? The hunters are coming. You have to fight or Rune and I will be killed."

Again, Ulf shook his head. There was pain in his eyes, so tangible that I looked for his wound. But I found only old white scars on his front legs, big areas bare of hair where once he'd been bitten by a monster who looked like him. He'd been afraid last night when he'd almost killed a man. He wouldn't do it again.

"I get it, Ulf," I said quietly. "I see you." I walked over and put my hand on a scar on his front leg, to show him I understood.

He sighed deeply.

I turned back to Dag. "We have to run deeper into the woods. They won't track us forever. We can find somewhere to hide, somewhere defensible."

"Oh, is that what we *must* do, little brother?" Dag's voice was sarcastic. He didn't sound like himself. The sharp edge of anger twisted like a dagger in his side.

"What is wrong with you?"

"I just notice you've taken charge lately. I'm wondering

why, when you never had any interest in anything but books and sitting around before."

It was a valid question. I'd noticed it myself. I felt an urgency to be sure things were done right that I'd never felt before, although frankly, with how terribly everything was going, I wasn't sure I was doing any good at all.

"I don't care who's in charge. I care that no one gets hurt."

"Oh, I'd say they've hurt us," Dag said. His eyes roved over Gus's wolf body, which was covered in drying blood. "They backed the sorcerer who cursed us and took our sister. I'd say they fucking hurt us." He gripped his bow with a white fist. He would not run away.

"There's nothing to be gained by choosing violence," I said slowly.

"Then find a tree to scamper up," Dag said. "Find a hole to crawl into. I'm not running from this." He walked away from us all, back towards the village, towards the hunt.

"Please, go," I begged the wolves as I turned to follow Dag. "Ulf, you shouldn't have to fight. Gus, go with Ulf. We'll slow them down. They won't hurt us. We're men. It'll be okay. You should go."

Of course they fell into step behind me, their paws padding silently on the forest floor. We were brothers, after all. We stayed together.

We were not far outside the village when we met the party. While they'd ventured slowly, shuffling as a mass, Dag had charged forward with his long hunter's legs and now stood before them, his bow in his hand. Arrows at his back. Daggers in his eyes.

"Turn back," Dag said. "It is my brothers you have come to hunt and it won't stand." His shoulders were back and he seemed so strong, and yet I could see that he was about to shatter.

It was like the villagers couldn't hear him. With open mouths they looked up, up, at Gus and Ulf. The two wolves towered behind us. Their very bodies were weapons.

Dag drew an arrow and nocked it.

Our father pushed through the crowd to the front. He was sober. I'd learned to recognize the signs. The strange way he did not sway on his feet, and the way his hands shook. The lines around his eyes were of a man twice widowed. "Son, turn your weapon around. The wolves are right behind you. You can take the kill."

"Father." I stepped forward, raising my hands in a gesture of peace. "These wolves behind us are not the pack that has been after Marius' flock. They are Gus and Ulf, transformed by the sorcerer. You *saw* Gus turn yourself. You must not harm them, and they will not harm any of you either."

"Tell that to Arne!" someone shouted. "He's nearly dead!" A shiver went through the crowd.

"Ulf was afraid!" I called out. "He was cornered. He wouldn't hurt a fly on purpose. Disperse, and you will be perfectly safe."

"Son, get out of the way," my father said, and there was an axe in his hand. What on earth was he doing with that? Was he even strong enough to swing it? He hadn't lifted pigs onto the hooks in years. The muscles of his arms were withered with disuse.

"Father, no, these are your sons! Igor did this, and you saw.

You *saw* Gus change! How can you not remember?"

"I re-remember," he slurred, and stumbled. I knew with a sinking heart that he was not sober after all. He had picked up a bottle between Igor's tower and the woods. It hardly mattered. He wasn't on our side, sober or drunk.

He looked right at Dag. "You pig. You swine. You're not fit to live in my house! You might as well be hanging on the hook with the rest of them." He gestured widely, as if all the village were made of pigs, and almost tipped over.

Dag raised his bow and pulled the string back to his ear. His face was dead calm.

"Dag," I said shakily. "Dag, put that down. What are you doing?"

You swine, our mother had called him. *You little shit. You're not worth the food it takes to feed you.*

"Dag—"

Our father had never once tried to stop her. No one had except the two wolves who stood behind Dag now.

"Stand down!" Dag screamed. "You can't have them too! You can't! You can't do this to us! I won't stand for it!"

"Put 'em down!" From deep in a barrel chest the call of the blacksmith came, resonant and sure. The crowd raised their weapons and cried out. They surged forward.

"Stand down!" Dag called again, loud and final. "Stand down or else I swear—"

"Please, don't! Don't!" I cried. Ulf and Gus growled, bending their front legs and assuming postures of readiness.

But the villagers came.

And Dag let his arrow fly.

Our father grunted. The arrow stuck proudly in his chest

and the villagers, who'd been crowding around him, backed away as one as he fell to his knees. His eyes were confused. His shaking hands found the shaft and felt about, as if trying to figure out what happened to him. Was he too numb to feel the wound, or was he in agony? Could he understand that it was his own son who'd shot him?

I ran to him. One hand cushioned his back and the other found his on the arrow. Blood seeped from the wound, which was straight through his heart. Already his eyelids fluttered, and he tipped. I held him upright.

"Dag," I breathed. "Dag, what have you done?" I looked at my brother's face, expecting it to mirror my own. I'd see horror at what he'd done. Shock. He wouldn't be able to believe it.

"My finger slipped," he'd say, coming forward and sinking to his knees. He'd regret this moment every day for the rest of his life.

But that is not what I saw.

Dag's face was a sneer, his lip curling back violently, his eyes spitting scorn. "Anybody else?" he cried, nocking another arrow.

The crowd jostled each other in their rush to run away.

But Dag's eyes picked out the bully in the crowd who'd punched him last night. An arrow flew and found its target. Dag could hit a squirrel through the eye at a hundred paces. His arrow hit the man in the back of the head and slid out his left eye in a mess of pus and blood. The man's knees made a horrible, heavy cracking sound as they hit the ground. Then he tipped forward and the ground shoved the arrow point backwards. Its feathers stuck up straight in the air, its shaft covered in blood.

I couldn't speak. I couldn't breathe. Vaguely, as if from far away, I heard barking. Gus and Ulf. "Stop, stop," they said with their new voices. But Dag nocked another arrow.

My hands were wet where they pressed against our father's chest. He wheezed and his eyelids fluttered. His heartbeat slowed under my hand. Without a final word, he passed. The heaviness took him and his shoulders drooped, and his body was the weight of death in my hands. I pressed my palms against him tighter so he would not fall. Slowly, I lowered him to the ground.

Something tickled my cheek and I brushed it away. A tear.

"That's right, get out," roared Dag. His voice was huge. It filled the woods. It echoed in the caves and the crevasses of hollow trees. Squirrels scampered away; birds and sprites fled.

And the hunters fled too. They ran as fast as they could back to the safety of their homes and hearths.

When they were gone, and the woods were empty of all but us and the bodies of the men Dag killed, I turned to my brother. Tears flowed freely down my face, and the emotions in me could not be named. Not grief, for I'd had little love for my father. Not rage. Not even, though it was hard to admit, was it shock. I thought of the whispers I'd overheard between Dag and Cat on that day they'd made love in the tree house. Yes, this had always been in him. But he'd fought against it and won, all his life. Until he didn't.

Dag's face was triumphant, satisfied.

"Dag," I said. I was quiet, but my voice was the biggest thing in the woods. "Dag, how could you?"

A frown furrowed Dag's brow, and for a moment he looked confused. He looked past me to our father's body, and considered for a moment if what he'd done might be horrible. I watched him discard the possibility like a scarf when the sun comes out.

"Dag—"

"What, Rune?" He made my name sound like an insult. "Are you going to pretend now that he's dead that our father was some hero? That he was even a good man?"

"No, I'm not, but *you* were a good man."

Dag shrugged this off.

"What about him?" I gestured at the young man who'd done nothing to deserve his arrow.

"Lanzo was a bully. He came for our family, Rune, twice. Do you have no loyalty? Do you think I should've just let him kill us?" Dag's voice was coldly practical, but he paced as if the energy pent up in him was too much. He needed to pour it out. More killing might sate him, though I couldn't imagine how much it would take. I did not even know this man before me.

"Dag, I know you're upset—"

Dag laughed, harsh and mocking. "Upset? Upset, Rune?" He leapt forward. His eyes were yellow in the sunlight, when once they'd been brown. His hair blew back, revealing the tips of his ears, which were pointed. "Of course I'm upset! That freak stole our sister! He sent our own father out to kill us. He did—" he pointed "—*this* to our brothers!"

"Your ears," I said unsteadily. "Dag, your eyes. You look like him. Like Igor. You're changing too."

But Dag shook this away as nonsense. He began to pace again, to leave what I'd said behind. "I'm nothing like him, Rune. He's a fucking monster."

My sad eyes drank in the shape of the man who was once the kindest I knew. "But you are, Dag. Look at what you've done. *You* are a monster."

Dag's eyes bulged in his head.

And then, my words having swept some prophecy into motion, Dag's pointed ears grew fur. His body lengthened and he grew tall. His body snapped his bow with a loud crack and splinters flew. Dag roared his rage and fear and pain as the changes took him.

I knew what was happening. I closed my eyes so that I wouldn't have to see it again. When I opened them, the result was what I'd expected. Three beasts shaped like wolves looked back at me with yellow eyes.

CHAPTER 14

WE WENT TO the tree house. I led us there, I think. I was in a daze.

When we arrived, I realized that I was the only one light enough to climb up onto the platform to sleep. I looked at my brothers in apology. Except Dag. I couldn't look at Dag.

"I wasn't thinking," I said.

I felt so tired, my head was a fog. There was iron in my limbs, and I could barely lift them to put one leg and then the other on the rungs of the ladder that took me up to the platform where, only days ago, I'd accidentally overheard a tender moment between Cat and Dag.

I took off my cloak and laid it out as a bed. I lay on the uneven planks, the roughness of Ulf's early work digging into my back. I fell instantly to sleep.

I woke at dusk to strange sounds from below. The sky was purple like a bruise, the pain of the dying day smudged above the pines. A sharp board at my back reminded me where I was.

"Ulf? Gus?" I stumbled to the ladder. My body, still thick

with sleep, slipped on the rungs as I tried to be quick. "Ulf, Gus, Dag," I whisper-shouted, unsure if we were alone.

What did I hear? A sound like the squeal of an animal in pain.

I followed it and found them. Like creatures from a nightmare, their bodies were stretched and malformed. A human hand stuck out from a hairy foreleg. A tiny hairless ear was dwarfed by a giant yellow eye. They were changing back.

When men stood before me again, I sank to my knees and uttered a prayer of thanks. I'd not thought to ever see their faces again.

But it wasn't quite their faces. In the falling light, three sets of yellow eyes peered down at me. Three sets of pointed ears. And pointed teeth.

"You look like him," I told them. My voice sounded tired, and I was sorry to be the one to say it, but I was the only one who could see all three. They looked at each other, leaning forward, peering in the failing light, and they saw. They saw what I meant.

"Shit," Gus said quietly. He touched his own face, feeling for the points of his teeth and the strange new shape at the top of his ears. "Shit, shit."

"It doesn't matter," Dag said. He stood stiffly, refusing to feel about and discover himself like the others. "It's the least important thing."

Ulf nodded his agreement, his hands dropping back to his sides. "Yeah. At least we're not wolves anymore. Why do you think it wore off?"

The moon glowed above our heads, only a sliver. The new moon. I stood and tilted my head back to study it.

"I don't think it wore off."

"What do you mean?" Gus asked.

"I don't know for sure. But…in my stories, when people are enchanted, they take a false shape during the day and turn back into themselves at night. It's dusk right now. I won't know if I'm right until…" I drifted off.

"Until morning," Ulf finished. He shuddered. "You think we'll turn back into wolves again."

I nodded.

"What the fuck is this curse he cast?" Dag demanded.

Each of my brothers was naked. Ulf and Gus, always big men, looked about the same to me, besides the changes to their faces. But Dag had changed more. He looked bigger, his shoulders larger and hunched forward. He looked ready to charge, to crouch, to strike.

"Gus and I were talking about it before…" I swallowed and kept on. "In that maze at Igor's tower, what did you see, Ulf?"

"Aurora was there. She was holding Greta right in front of me, and Igor was nowhere around. I stepped forward to grab her, and a whole pack of wolves appeared from nowhere. They tore Greta from Aurora's arms and—" His face was pale, and he stopped speaking. He swallowed. "But that's not all. Then, somehow, I was the wolf. I was the one tearing Greta apart, and I couldn't stop."

As one, we shuddered. "Dag?" I asked.

Dag's whole body was stiff. He tossed his hair off his face but did not speak. His mouth was a thin line across his face. He would not tell, but I did not need him to.

"Igor showed us each different visions, individual visions

according to our fears, and he told us to become what we feared most. For Ulf, it was an obvious one. He became a wolf almost right away. For the rest of us…"

I tapered off. It felt mean somehow to point at my brother's fears and blame them for their fates. But they looked at me with questioning eyes, not getting it. They needed me to explain. "For the rest of us, our fears weren't so physical. I think maybe this curse craves a material form. Did you see Igor rubbing that tooth when he cast it? It's a wolf's tooth. Maybe the curse has…preferences. It tries to find its way to a physical punishment."

"It tries?" Dag sneered. "You make it sound sentient."

"Look, I don't know about curses," I said sharply. "I'm guessing. Do you have a better guess?"

Dag shut up.

"Ulf was easy. Gus, a little harder. Gus was helpless to get Aurora back before he became a wolf, but it's worse now. He changed right at the moment when changing would deprive him of every advantage he had left."

"What about Dag?" Gus asked.

Dag stood straight, head held high. Proud eyes dared me to analyze him, to explain him away into a little box. "And you, Rune?" he sneered. "Do you fear nothing? Is that what we're meant to believe?"

"No. No, of course I do."

Dag held out his arms, encompassing me. *Then why are you still a man?* they asked. An accusation.

"I don't know why I haven't changed yet. I'm fairly sure I will. The curse is just waiting for the right moment."

"I agree with Dag," Gus said. "A curse can't be sentient,

Rune. It doesn't make sense."

I shrugged. "Maybe I'm wrong. I only tell you what I see. Aurora would know better than me. All I know of magic is what I've read in stories."

"We have to get her back," Ulf said. "No matter what happens to us. We can't leave her with him."

It was the only thing left that we agreed on, so we walked back to the village. But in the hours we slept, it had utterly changed.

"What is that?" I said as we approached.

Dag began to run, out-pacing the rest of us. He sprinted forward and came back to report. "It's a fence," he said grimly.

"What?" Gus said, as Ulf said, "How?"

I ran to see for myself.

Yes, it was a fence, and there was no explanation other than that Igor had helped erect it. Wooden fence posts were buried deep in the ground. A rough wooden structure passed between them, and filling in all the gaps were brambles. Thorns protruded in all directions, sharp as needles.

Ulf slammed his shoulder against one of the fence posts. It didn't budge. Thorns cut his arm and blood ran down his skin. He picked the thorns out and tossed them away.

Then he reached for his axe. He lifted it above his head in a practiced swing. He brought it down in a perfect arc onto the vines. They sliced clean and parted.

Gus congratulated Ulf, a hand on his shoulder, but I was watching the fence. "Look!"

The brambles writhed and twisted like living snakes. They coiled over each other, crawling into the space we'd made. As they slithered, the thorns lengthened. The vines thickened.

Down the fence, the growth traveled like a wave until all the fence that we could see was engorged.

Ulf raised his axe again.

"Don't," I cried, but he swung again. He hit the same spot, and the brambles fell away again beneath his blade. But just as quickly, the fence responded. Twisting and coiling, it squeezed itself tighter until there were hardly any gaps and the thorns were as big as thumbs.

"Come on," I said. "Let's look for a gate."

My brothers nodded, Dag swearing under his breath.

We began a slow circle around the fence. We wove between trees that grew close to it, their branches and leaves draped over the top.

As we circled, an unease came over me. I could not name the reason until we'd come all the way around again to where we started.

"Cat's house is inside the fence," I said. It bothered me for her to be trapped in there when she so loved the woods.

I looked at Dag. Did it bother him too?

But he was focused elsewhere. It was like he'd forgotten her. Or the man who'd loved her was gone. "There's no gate," he said. "There's no way in."

"Or out," Ulf noted.

"Maybe it's invisible. Maybe he hid it somehow," Gus said. "Maybe this whole fence is an illusion."

"A good one," Ulf said, flexing his arm, which was spotted with tiny blood dots.

"There *must* be a gate," I said. "Think of the market. All those out-of-towners who come to sell wares. The mayor was trying to grow the town. They can't *possibly* allow Igor to change them so much, to block them off from the outside world completely." But even I didn't believe this. The truth was clear.

All that was left out here was woods and monsters.

"We should knock," Gus said stubbornly. "Knock and shout. We grew up here. This is *our* village. Someone will hear us and let us in."

We waited until the earliest light of pre-dawn lit the forest in pinks and purples. Gus stood near a tiny gap in the fence, through which he could see cottages. He waited until women walked the streets. He shouted until his voice was hoarse. He shouted until his face lengthened into a snout, and he could shout no more.

Nobody inside even looked up.

Perhaps the wall was enchanted to block sound. Perhaps the villagers were simply too far to hear. Or perhaps they ignored him on purpose.

We could not know.

But they turned when he howled. Horrified, they turned to the invisible woods. They clutched each other and gathered their children to their sides and disappeared into the center of the village. A village that no longer belonged to us.

We were their monsters now. We were the stuff of their nightmares.

CHAPTER 15

WE WERE MONSTERS trapped in a nightmare, but we could not give up. When Ulf changed, his cuts became pinpricks buried beneath fur. He began immediately to slam himself against the fence again. Under the weight of his massive body, the fence posts creaked and leaned. He retreated, his chest and shoulders bleeding from fresh cuts. He slammed himself forward again and again. The fence wavered, bending.

Gus and Dag joined him. Their blood splattered the forest floor, peppering green leaves with red. Brambles snapped and posts tilted. The entire thing groaned as a single fence post cracked. And then, the vines began to writhe like before. They wound themselves around weakened fence posts, propping them back up. The entire fence thickened and grew taller, reaching for the open sky. When it encountered tree branches, it simply enveloped them and kept going.

And the thorns. Oh, the thorns, they grew. They grew from the size of my thumb to the size of my forearm, until Dag yipped and drew back, and Gus howled and drew back, and together they barked at Ulf until he drew back, soaked in blood.

My heart pounded with worry when I saw his wounds. Weak and limping, he walked to a river and washed. The blood made the water run red. Some of the wounds were very deep.

I was the only one of us who was human and could treat him, but what could I do? I had no cloth to wrap his wounds. I had no sutures to sew them shut. I had only the bounty of the woods, and I was the least qualified of us to make use of it.

I chose a clean spot on the ground. "Lie down," I said, pointing. They'd told me they could still understand me when I spoke, even in their wolf form.

Ulf obeyed.

I tore off my shirt and pressed it to the deepest of the cuts in his chest. I leaned all my weight against it to stop the bleeding.

Gradually, it worked.

But what more could I do? I wished desperately for Aurora to be with us. Her skills were needed now more than ever. But we had yet to get her back.

That night my brothers changed to men again, and the first thing I did was run to Ulf to see his wounds.

He looked like a man who'd been whipped. His entire front was raw and red. Most cuts were shallow, but there were two that worried me. One thorn had pierced deep into his gut. I could not know if it had punctured anything important, but I did know that it needed to be sewn and treated to prevent infection. The other was a jagged slice along his collarbone. The edges were rough and raw. I picked tiny prickers from it with my fingertips as Ulf groaned beneath my ministrations. "Even the thorns have thorns," I muttered. I thought there might still be more in there, and I knew it would not heal clean.

Gus, Dag and I spoke as Ulf rested. They, too, were cut up, but not so badly. They had not pummeled themselves against the wall with Ulf's fierceness. They had not kept on until they'd nearly died.

"Do you think you could jump it as a wolf?" I asked.

Dag scoffed. "Did you see how high it is now?"

"The more we tried to get past it, the more it grew."

I nodded. "We have to be smarter. We can't use force against it. We have to try something else."

Every day and every night we considered what that should be. A fever took Ulf, and he tossed and turned, forehead red. I circled the wall over and over, staring up at the trees that had been half-swallowed by it. Thinking that maybe, if I were a wolf, I could jump it. But I had not changed.

Days later, I spotted a convoy approaching the village. It was market day tomorrow. I'd forgotten. I watched from the shadows of the trees as they approached the village. They stared in awe at the wall of brambles that surrounded Baneswood. They went off the path, seeking a gate, but they found nothing and turned back, their carts still laden with wares.

When night fell, Gus and Dag approached their camp with weapons and stole their carts away. I ripped apart the contents, hoping for something to help Ulf, but I found nothing.

"He's getting worse," I told my brothers. "I don't know what to do."

"Aurora would know what to do," Gus said firmly.

"I know," I said quietly, "but she's not here."

We needed her. We needed to save her so she could save us.

"I have an idea," Dag said, "but it's suicidal."

"Tell me," Gus and I said at once.

"We jump the fence."

"You said you couldn't," I objected. "You said it was too high."

"I thought of a way. We climb trees as men. The three of us. There are plenty that overhang the fence. We climb one as men, wait to change, then we drop into the village once we turn."

"I don't turn," I reminded him.

"You can sit on my back to make the drop," Dag said.

"Then what?" Gus asked. "How do we take Aurora? How do we get back out?"

Dag's voice was slick and quiet, like the blade of a dagger silently leaving its sheath to bury itself in the flesh of a man's belly. "We walk over and take her. We overpower anyone who stops us. We are big bad wolves now, remember? I dare the coward to stand against us."

"We might have to hurt innocent people," I said, even though I was not the one who would do the hurting.

"So be it," said Dag and Gus at once.

"And we still don't know how we'll get back out."

"You think the fence has thorns like that on the inside? No way. We'll slam against it until it lets us out. We'll tear the limbs off that evil little man until he makes us a door. I don't know how we get out and I don't care. This is how we get in."

It was all the plan we had. And so Gus, Dag and I climbed a tree.

Just after dawn, we dropped, me on Dag's back. I fell off and thudded hard on the ground. I rose, rubbing my shoulder. "I'm okay," I whispered, but they hadn't waited to see. Gus and Dag were already running ahead through the empty streets, which would soon fill.

I turned back to look at the fence on this side. It was as smooth as Dag thought it would be. Delicate branches of ivy crept along a wooden frame. Aurora and I could climb it until we reached a low-hanging branch, then climb down on the other side. Dag and Gus could hide until they changed and then do the same. Or maybe if they battered the fence on this side, it wouldn't fight back.

I went along behind, slower but more stealthily. I pulled a hood around my head and hoped that casual passersby would not look at my face.

The village was already changed. Once, squirrels skittered across the streets seeking fallen fruit from the market. Now there was an eerie stillness. Birds did not sing. A veil of magic had fallen over the whole place, as if when Igor stifled my sister's voice, he'd muzzled the soul of the whole town.

We'll get Aurora and Greta. I'll get them out, and Aurora will help Ulf, and it'll all be okay.

I clung to this fantasy, for I still would not imagine a world where it all didn't go right. I fingered the vial of poison in my pocket.

We arrived at the apothecary's tower without waking anyone, but the door was still too small for my brothers to pass through without struggle. They slammed their shoulders against it, again and again. The hollow pounding sound echoed in the empty air, but no birds alighted from trees to fly away. They were already gone.

The door crashed open and we squeezed into the shop. It was empty. The stairs leading upstairs were too small for them to climb, and I realized I'd have to go upstairs alone.

My blood was cold with memory. In my visions, I'd climbed these stairs only to pierce Greta with a knife. No matter what I did, it ended poorly.

This was a terrible plan. It was no plan at all, really.

Trying for silence, I crept up the stairs. They creaked on seemingly every step, and my heart fluttered and raced.

Would I find the apothecary at the top, sleeping next to my sister in his bed?

Was this moment even real?

My sister was in bed alone. Igor was not here. Neither, it seemed, was Greta. The cradle from my vision was empty.

Aurora slept, seemingly peaceful, and I hesitated.

I wished, of course, to see her blink her eyes open and smile at me. "Rune," she'd say warmly, or sadly, or whatever she felt, and she'd hug me hello. But it was more likely she would try to stop me from taking her. It was safer to carry her downstairs still asleep.

But she was already waking. Her blue eyes blinked open. She smiled at me, and my heart broke open and hope tumbled out.

"Rune," she said, rising in the bed. "You came. I've missed you. Why did you imprison me up here and never visit?"

I swallowed the lump in my throat. "I didn't imprison you. Igor did. We have to go now. He might come back at any time. We have to get you out of here."

She looked puzzled, and then I saw it: the corners of her mouth were working strangely again, as if she chewed an invisible bit. Her eyes shifted through a collage of emotions, one moment sleepy, the next enraged, and the next softly innocent, like she had no idea what was going on.

"Why, I'm not leaving," she said. "How silly for you to think I would." A cruel smile overtook her face, and her tone changed. She sounded like *him* now. "How childish of you, after what happened the last time you tried to take me."

A heavy ball of dread settled in my stomach. Downstairs, a wolf yipped. But I did not know if it was a warning or a question about what was going on up here.

I took a tentative step towards the bed. "Aurora," I said slowly. I held up my hands to show I meant no harm. In truth, I had no idea what would cause harm anymore. The world had twisted and turned, made neighbor into enemy and brother into monster and sister into foe. "We are going downstairs. I'd prefer you come with me voluntarily, but I will take you, if I have to."

She laughed, like him, and threw off the covers. She stood in her nightgown and stretched. Her eyes spit sparks of fire as they settled on me. A demented smile carved her face.

She opened a drawer on her nightstand and retrieved Gus's cleaver. She held it loosely in her hand. She lifted it to her face and caressed herself with the flat side of the blade. Down her cheek, her neck, her breast.

My blood was ice and fire. I breathed so fast, I began to feel dizzy.

"Try it," Aurora said softly.

My visions had already shown me what would happen if I

did. We would struggle until she stabbed herself with the blade. I would lose her forever.

I breathed in and out, heavy and fast. I was frozen in place at the moment of the decision.

I never wanted to have to make these kinds of decisions! My mind screamed angrily, and Aurora smiled as if she could hear.

Taking the cleaver with her, she climbed back into bed. She pulled the covers over herself and lay down to go back to sleep. "Goodbye, Rune," she said, but one corner of her mouth was trying to stop smiling. It was trying to turn down, and the result was an incessant twitch.

She was still in there fighting. I *knew* it.

I realized suddenly that Igor's nightmare visions were a gift. They'd taught me all the things that would not work. Like the fence—if I applied force, I would only make things worse. But there was another way.

"Aurora," I said, "I know you're in there. The real you. It's Rune, and downstairs there's Gus and Dag. Ulf is in the woods. He's injured, and we need your help to save his life. If you come with me, I'll take you to Ulf. I'll take you away from Igor. If you just come with me, I promise he won't touch you ever again."

Was it another promise I couldn't keep? It couldn't be. I would die trying to keep it.

My sister was frozen. Her pose stiffened, and then began to vibrate as if she shook from the inside. A rough voice squeezed out of her, its tone high and strange. "Nice try, boy. But she's mine."

No, no, she wasn't his. She was her own, and she was fighting. I watched the battle take place before me. My words had inflamed Aurora's fight, and she was struggling to free herself.

The world narrowed to this moment. No past, no future.

I felt the vial of poison against my leg like a rock in my pocket. I dug my hand in to take it out. My fingers shaking, I popped the stopper from the vial.

"You know what this is," I said quietly. The stiff, shaking creature before me nodded, barely perceptible, and I knew it was the real Aurora who had done it. "It's your poison," I said anyway, so that *he* would know too. "It's deadly. And Aurora, if you don't come with me right now, I'm going to drink it."

On the night she was taken, I picked up this weapon and had yet to find a way to use it. Now I found the only way. My visions had shown me that Igor used people like shields. Every move I made against him sacrificed someone else. So I would risk only myself.

I raised the vial close to my lips. *Does it give off a scent? If I breathe in too deeply, will I drop down dead?*

"Aurora, since the moment you were born, we brothers cared for you. Your mother was dead, and Father was in the bottle, and it was just us five."

She was shaking harder now, shuddering as if she'd fallen in an icy winter pond, and all I wished was to rush to her side and throw a blanket around her, but I stayed standing still and speaking quietly. The magic of love was the only weapon I had left.

"You must've felt so alone and scared these last days. I'm so sorry. We tried to rescue you. We've tried since the minute you were taken. We love you, Aurora. Come back to us. Come back, because if you can't, we're not anything. If you can't, I won't go on without you."

I touched the edge of the vial to my lips. My hands weren't shaking anymore. I was utterly calm. I had no thoughts. Below us, in the main shop, a wolf barked, then growled.

"You're stronger than him," I whispered. "You are. Break his spell on you."

Aurora shook so hard she dropped the cleaver. She fell back on the bed, seizing, and still I did not go to her. Still I stood locked in place, waiting with poison on my lips.

"Go!" she screamed, an ugly, hateful sound. At first I thought she was speaking to me, but then I noticed her eyes, which were looking into a mirror. She raised herself to her elbows, her eyes hardened steel. "Go! Get out of here! Go!"

Fierce wind whistled and a rush of air nearly tipped the vial over into my mouth. Aurora collapsed on the bed, shuddering. With shaking fingers, I stoppered the vial. I rushed to Aurora and held her in my arms.

"Aurora, is it you? Is it you?"

My sister, pale and sweating, looked up at me. She did not smile. It was her. Relief fluttered in me like a dove, and I said a silent prayer of gratitude.

"We have to go now, before Igor comes back."

"But I can't go," my sister said, her voice anguished.

I felt cold. "Greta?"

She began to sob, feral heaving moans. I held her, clutching her to me. Her arms went around me and she screamed, a deep groan of agony, and I realized that this was all too little, too late. But my mind clung stubbornly to the plan.

"Come on. Come on, get up. Come on, Aurora, get up. We'll get her back too; I swear it. Just get up."

I stood, and she took the vial from my hands and placed it into her pocket so that I could take her into my arms. I rushed down the stairs.

"He's not here," I told my brothers. "I've got her. Her enchantment is broken, but Greta isn't here with her."

We couldn't discuss the problem. We couldn't decide together what to do. I alone had to make the decision.

"We've got to get her out of here before Igor comes back."

Dag was out the door in an instant. Gus waited behind, bending down so that I could deposit Aurora onto his back. She clutched his fur and continued to sob.

Out we went into the street, and down it towards the fence.

"Aurora," I called to her. I raced to keep pace with Gus. "Is there a door in the fence?"

"He wouldn't let me leave the house," she said quietly. So she didn't know. But I knew someone who would.

Villagers filled the streets. They screamed as they saw us, dropping baskets and abandoning carts. They clutched their children to them and ran for cover in their houses, closing and bolting doors. I did not see Igor, but he must be here somewhere. We *had* to get out before he found us.

"To Cat's," I called, and Dag shifted direction, Gus following.

Nobody engaged us. We flew past them, but I was sure they ran right to Igor. Igor, who still had Greta.

My heart pounded and I did not know at all if I was doing the right thing. I knew only that I *must* get Aurora out. She would go save Ulf, and I would stay behind for Greta. That was my new plan.

We were coming up on Cat's house. Yes, as I suspected, her father's fields sat at the very edge of Baneswood now. She could open her bedroom shutters and reach out to touch the thorns.

"Cat," I screamed. "Cat!"

Dag barked loudly, yapping over and over.

"Cat!" I screamed over his noise. And there she was, flinging open the door, her long brown hair flowing free, wavy. Her bow was on her shoulder, her tattoo standing out on her pale arm. She nocked an arrow and pointed it at the wolf.

"No! Cat, no! It's Dag! It's Dag!" I waved my hands, and her eyes flew to me. Her bow lowered. Relief swept through me at this miracle: that of all the villagers, she had not fallen under Igor's spell.

I raced to her, slamming into her as I failed to slow. "Cat. The fence. Is there a gate? A door? A way out?!" I shook her, not meaning to.

Her big eyes took in Aurora on Gus's back. "Oh," she murmured. How much had she even known of what was happening? "No. No, there's no gate." Her small hands gripped my arms back, tightly, and I felt her fear. She was caught in this cage too, I realized. She was a trapped animal now too.

"But—" She hesitated, looking over my brothers again.

"It's Gus and Dag," I said quietly. "Igor cursed them. He kidnapped my sister. He still has Greta. Please, Cat, help us."

"But Rune, it's not much help," she said miserably. "Only I kept a small hole open while the fence was going up. I shoved a big rock into place, and if you roll it out and dig a little, you'll be able to go through. None of the vines grew there. Only—"

She drifted off, eying my brothers, towering monsters.

"Only it's just big enough for a man."

"If that," she whispered.

I knew too that it would close as soon as I took the rock out. I'd seen it before.

"I'll get Aurora through," I said, projecting confidence, although really my mind raced. My brothers were trapped here until night, and surely they'd be found before then. Would I still have brothers left living by the time night came? "It's all we have. Thank you, Cat." I took her hands and squeezed. I tried to be gentle.

'That's Dag?" she whispered, looking past me at her lover.

I felt so reluctant to tell her. "He's changed," I said. "But... not just on the outside."

"He killed your father. And Lanzo. I heard."

Her frown was a tragedy on her face, a vision of confusion and betrayal.

"Igor cursed us, Cat. It's not Dag's fault. He changed Dag..." But even as I said these things to rid my brother of responsibility for what he'd done, I didn't really believe them. "Where's the way out? We need to get Aurora out now."

But Aurora was dismounting. She was wiping her tears and looking back towards the village proper. "Greta. We *have* to go back for Greta. I'm not leaving without her."

I clenched my jaw and went to her.

"You have to. Do you understand, Aurora? You have to, or else you'll never get out."

"Then I'll never get out. She's my daughter, Rune. She's my daughter!" She moved to run back and I grabbed her arm to make her turn towards Cat's house instead.

"Show me," I demanded, and Cat, though she looked at me queerly, as if perhaps it was not only Dag who had changed, ran around the back of her house.

"He didn't walk back here, so he didn't see," she said. There was a large boulder at the base of the ivy. A wolf could easily push it out of the way, but a wolf could not fit between her house and the wall.

Swearing, I let go of Aurora's arm. "Wait here," I said. I glared around the house at Gus, telling him with my eyes to watch her, make sure she didn't try to run away. I tried to move the stone. Cat joined me. We pushed and we shoved. "How did you do this on your own?" I asked her, and she smiled at the compliment. She ran to get a digging bar and we levered the boulder out of the way.

Aurora had darted out of my sight. I knew that Gus would not let her run away, but I knew too that once the stone was moved, it would not be long before the ivy grew to cover the space. I went around the house after her, and breathed a sigh of relief when I saw her. She stood still in her nightgown, my brothers before her.

But they were not facing her. They were facing away, growling.

I shifted to see past them, and there he was.

The apothecary, with villagers ranged around him like an army. Were they all under his spell?

I stepped forward into the hate that filled their eyes. The same as in his. The same as in ours. We were all consumed by it now.

But what was that in his arms? It emitted a tiny wail, and my blood turned to ice in my veins. My sister raised her head and sobbed. She looked lost and small, and yet determined too, her spine an iron rod down her back. She held out her arms, her fingers spread wide.

"Give her to me."

Igor's fingers clenched on his prize. And I knew that he would never let that child go, not in a thousand years, and if we tried to take her, we'd lose my sister too.

The decision yawned before me like a chasm, my childhood on one side and a man full of regret on the other. As in my visions, I was the one with the choice. It all rode on my shoulders.

I could drag Aurora away. Gus and Dag could attack, distracting Igor, and I could shove Aurora into the small hole Cat had kept open and out into the free world.

But without Greta, Aurora would never really be free.

And my brothers would be left behind.

Or we could fight. I could watch my brothers massacre the villagers who were like family. I could watch the sorcerer recapture my sister's mind, this time forever.

My eyes sought his hands. Did he carry his tooth between his fingers? No, it was around his neck on its cord. His hands were holding Greta. So long as he held her, he could not clutch his talisman and pierce his fingers and cast a curse. I must not allow him to put Greta down.

The moment yawned. The future waited.

I looked the sorcerer in the eye. And I saw something. Was it nervousness? He glanced at Dag and Gus as if, for once, he was not in control. He was not laughing, not smiling with cocky pride.

I remembered his retreat to the stairs when Gus changed to

a wolf and got too close. A suspicion formed, one unfounded.
There was only one way to test it. Only one way out.

I looked over at Cat. Her fearful eyes met mine. "Get
Aurora through that hole," I told her quietly.

"I'm coming with you," Cat whispered. "I can't live in
here."

My heart swelled and I nodded imperceptibly. "You'll find
Ulf near the tree house," I said.

Cat frowned. "Aren't you coming?"

I turned away, back to Igor. I met his eyes. Then I closed
mine.

And I let the terror flood into me. The fates of all those I
loved hung on my decision in this moment. I must be a man
instead of a boy, and make the choice that would doom or
save us all. Ah, my deepest fear, hello.

I made the choice, and the curse answered.

My nose lengthened until I could see it. I grew taller and
taller, a giant amongst men and monsters. A tail sprouted from
my back and I fell forward, catching myself with massive
claws. My clothes shredded around me and became tangled in
my legs, which bent strangely at the knee. Hair coated my body,
and my vision sharpened. My hearing sharpened. A mouse
nibbled biscuit crumbs in a nearby cottage. Fruit pits rotted in
the warm spring morning.

I was a wolf.

Gus? I thought. *Dag?*

Rune. You finally decided to join us, Gus answered. *What's the
move?*

*I don't think he can control our minds when we're wolves. He looks
afraid of us.*

He does, Dag confirmed.

As long as he's holding Greta, he can't touch his talisman.

So what do we do? Gus asked again.

There's a hole open behind the house, just small enough to fit Aurora and Cat. I told Cat to get Aurora through. We just have to distract Igor.

Aurora won't go without Greta, Gus said.

Then we get Greta.

CHAPTER 16

IGOR COULDN'T USE his magic against wolves.

I only suspected this, yet based on this guess I'd allowed the curse to make me a wolf.

Why would he turn us into something he couldn't control? I had no answer. But then, magic always did have a cost in the stories.

Igor held Greta before him like a shield, the villagers ranged about him as a personal army.

I jumped forward, darting around Aurora and my brothers. My new body was powerful and fast. In a moment I was beside the sorcerer. I lashed out, snapping at Igor's legs with my new big teeth, and Igor stumbled back. A glimpse of his face showed terror, and a thrill flew through me.

No vision had clouded my mind. No warped time. No cocky smile filled his face.

I was right. Igor's magics didn't work on wolves, and if I'd truly aimed to crush him, I could have. But he was still holding the child.

"Greta." Aurora screamed and rushed forward.

But the villagers swelled to answer Igor's need. A pitchfork jabbed my side and I turned, growling, to confront the farmer who held it. I butted him with my head and he fell back. But Dag was not so restrained.

He jumped into the crowd, teeth gnashing. Where they closed, villagers fell. They stabbed at him, but he was quick and ruthless. Dag closed his jaw over a man, crushing him like a grape. His insides spilled out.

Dag! Dag, stop! We just need to get them away from him! Stop!

But even Gus had fallen to bloodlust. *They'll surround us,* he cried in my mind. Gus slammed his head into a woman who ran at him. She flew back and tumbled over herself as she hit the ground.

The baker's wife came at Dag with an axe, and he ripped off the arm that held it. She fell to the ground, screaming. A sickening crunch sounded as Dag threw the blacksmith against a cottage. The man did not stand back up.

They were coming at me too. I kept my mouth firmly closed, swiping out with my paw or my head to batter them away. But even then, my sharp claws cut. I carefully opened my mouth once to rip an axe out of someone's hand, but he moved and I grazed his hand. I felt a finger come off in my mouth and I spit it out, disgusted, as he screamed.

But the army began to scatter. Our path to Igor was opening up, and he saw it too. He began to stumble away, Greta clutched tight to him.

Aurora ran flat out towards them, Cat running behind her screaming, "Aurora! Aurora!"

Aurora's nightgown swept out behind her like a white cape.

She was swift in her bare feet, closing the distance between the aging, stumbling sorcerer and herself.

Gus saw where she was going and ran to support her. He tore the weapons from the hands of Igor's guards. He growled, and he was a terror to them, a monster.

The hole might already be closing, I thought worriedly, but there was nothing I could do but follow a mother who followed her daughter.

Aurora was almost to Igor. She reached out her arms as if she planned simply to crash into him and wrench her daughter from his arms.

But a villager was headed at her in a collision course. He held a staff in his hands. He raised it above his head, his eyes full of hate. It was like he didn't even recognize her. He screamed, a warrior's cry, and Aurora turned towards the sound. When she saw him, she frowned and stopped running, frozen in disbelief.

Because it was Marius. Cat's father ran at my sister like he meant to kill her, his shepherd's staff raised above his head.

I was too far away. My eye caught Igor's, and the triumph was back in his eyes again. He might not be able to control us wolves, but he had the village, and that was enough.

Aurora! I cried, and my brothers moved. Dag was closest. He leapt—a gigantic, terrific jump over the heads of half a dozen villagers. They stabbed up at him with their weapons, but they only grazed him as he flew over them. His mouth opened as he landed, and Cat's scream, high-pitched and horrible, drowned out the sound of Marius' leg crunching as Dag's mouth closed over it.

Cat was a blur of fabric as she raced towards her father

and her lover. "Father! Father!"

Even Aurora was frozen, entranced by the violence, no longer moving towards Greta.

Dag shook his head, and Marius' leg ripped off at his hip. He collapsed, and blood spread rapidly around him. He did not scream. His pale face stared with wide eyes at his missing leg. He blinked, and his eyes closed.

"Father! Father!" Cat reached his side, skidding to her knees. Her shawl was coming off. She sought to wrap it around his wound, but there was no leg left to tie off. His entire hip was a gaping wound. She hiccuped with grief and shock, pressing her hands into the bleeding.

Her tear-streaked face found Aurora, silently appealing, but Aurora only watched in shock. Her skills could not heal this. Slowly, their heads turned towards Igor.

The triumph on his face as Aurora's beseeching gaze fell on him was unmistakable, and yet he sounded genuine when he said: "I'm sorry, my dear. This is beyond even my abilities."

Cat hiccuped again. I thought the bleeding was slowing. Marius' face was so pale. Cat felt for his pulse at his neck, her hand shaking. Then she sat back. She looked up at Dag, who stood above them, mouth dripping blood. And the hate in her eyes, oh, the hate.

"Stop this," Aurora said quietly. All eyes turned to her, but her eyes were still on Igor. "Stop this bloodshed."

"I know you grieve, but my dear, it was not I who did this." He dipped his chin at Marius' still form. He was still holding Greta, who was untouched by even a single blood drop.

"Yes it was, you know it was. But not only you." Aurora

looked at each of her brothers in turn, and I dipped my head in shame at what I saw in her gaze. Then she settled back on Igor. "I will make a deal with you."

His ears seemed to perk up. "Yes?"

"You let my brothers leave safely with Greta, and I will stay here with you."

"You would exchange yourself for your child?" His voice was so quiet. It was the first time I'd heard him admit that he knew that Aurora did not want him.

She nodded.

Igor barely hesitated. Right behind us, the ivy of the wall crawled away to create an opening big enough for even a monster to pass through. The wooden beams bent until they made an archway.

Aurora stepped towards Igor and nobody moved to stop her. She reached out for Greta, and he said, "But my dear, don't you wish us to raise your child? I assure you, I would raise her as if she were my own."

Aurora's mouth turned down. She spat on the ground and stared back at him with glaring hatred. Without answering, she took her daughter into her arms and carried her to the fence. She stepped through into the woods. Gently, with such love, she placed her daughter safely in the shade of a tree on the other side. She knelt with her. We could not hear what passed between them. What words of love she whispered. She kissed Greta's forehead and walked back, spine straight, tears streaking her face.

And maybe it was only I who saw her fingers clench a shape in the pocket of her nightdress. The vial of poison, which she'd taken from me in Igor's room.

My heart fell through my stomach.

Aurora had no intention of allowing the sorcerer to enchant her again. As soon as we were through the archway, she would drink it. She had exchanged her daughter's life for her own. This time, there would be no hope of rescue.

So another choice yawned before me. One that was perhaps not mine to make, and yet I *would* make it. Could I let Aurora carry out this suicide? Ulf might die as well if I did. But Greta would live safe with us, if Igor honored his word. He might come and try to take her back. If he did, we monsters would stop him.

It was what Aurora wanted.

But I could not abide it.

Aurora's stiff steps took her back to Igor's side. Her hand was in her pocket. Perhaps she'd unstoppered the vial already. Perhaps she had only moments left to live.

Igor looked positively joyful as she returned to his side. "Oh my dear," he gloated. "I knew you loved me. I just knew."

She did not even look at him. She looked at each of us in turn. For Dag, she had sadness. For Gus, resignation. I liked to imagine I saw love.

"Go. Take care of my daughter. Go."

None of us moved.

"Please. It's what I want."

When Igor heard this, he drew himself up and placed a hand on the small of her back. She twitched, then looked out at all the bloodshed.

"Go."

Gus whined. He came forward slowly, and Igor backed away, the ranks of his remaining army closing around him.

But Gus had only come to say goodbye. He pressed his head against Aurora's, and she closed her eyes and put one arm around him, hugging him to her. Her other hand did not leave her pocket.

Behind me in the woods, Greta wailed. It was the sound of my nightmares.

Gus walked through the archway and into the woods. He stood beside Greta beneath the shade of the tree.

Dag's eyes met Aurora's, and then settled on Cat. She still sat beside the body of her father, a pale form in a puddle of red. He too turned for the archway and retreated into the woods.

But I could not.

With shaking steps, I approached my sister. I bent my head to press against her stomach.

"Goodbye, Rune. Take good care of her," she whispered. Her hand was rising from her pocket, it was rising towards her mouth, a vial of glass clenched in her fist.

And so I opened my mouth and I closed it over her, gently. Teeth barely pricking her nightdress, I lifted her into the air. She screamed, and the liquid in the vial spilled out to splatter the ground.

Igor roared his rage. His hand ripped the tooth from around his neck. He held it out towards the fence and the archway collapsed. Quickly, so quickly, the wooden beams fell back into place and ivy grew to fill the spaces.

On the other side, my brothers barked.

Rune! Rune, run! Run!

I ran. I leapt villagers and raced towards the fence. I turned my head to the side so that Aurora would not be hurt when I smashed through the still-growing ivy.

The wooden beams shattered under my power. The vines broke, and we were through. Elation! We were on the other side. At my feet, Greta wailed, and at my sides, my brothers barked in joy and triumph.

I looked back through the hole, nearly closed. I met Cat's eyes where she sat beside her father. Sadness heavy in her eyes, she gave a little shake of her head. No, no she would not be coming with us after all.

My heart sank at that, but I had Aurora and I had Greta and Ulf would live after all. The villagers who raced towards us would not make it before the opening closed. There was only a tiny hole at the bottom now, hardly big enough for a child to pass through. We were safe.

But then, a rumble shook the earth. The fence—the entire thing—began to move. It swept towards us. On this side, it was still a tangle of razor-sharp thorns, thick as a man's arm, black and gleaming. They came at us like a hawk flying in for its prey, faster and faster.

Shit! Gus exclaimed, stumbling back.

Aurora was still in my mouth as she screamed, "Greta!" The wail pierced the air and my heart. Greta lay on the ground at the base of the tree, but none of us could safely pick her up. Only Aurora could.

As we watched in horror, the wall came for her. The opening passed right over Greta and she went through, unharmed. One moment she was there, and the next she'd been consumed by the village. The price for a broken deal.

Aurora screamed. Her arm stretched out towards the wall, and she struggled against me. If I put her down, she'd scrabble against the wall until it impaled her, trying to get through the hole, which was already closing. Not even small enough to swallow a baby anymore.

Run, I told my brothers. I turned with Aurora in my mouth. *Just run.*

Dag was already gone, a dart threading through the trees. Gus took off after him, and I followed last as the black wall of thorns hurdled at us, driving us deeper into our forest.

Finally, it stopped. I put Aurora down. We were close to the tree house and Ulf. When we approached him, he looked up, weak and hot, and Aurora ran to him and threw her arms around his neck. She was sobbing uncontrollably, her body wracked with grief. Then she swallowed her sobs to look at his wounds. She turned to Gus to request a specific flower. She told him where it grew. She built a fire and went up into the tree house to retrieve a pot she could boil water in, and only when this was all set did she turn to look at me.

Pinpricks of blood stained the stomach of her nightgown. I'd cut her after all.

Her eyes were dead orbs in her face, and her voice was monotone. "I'll never forgive you," she said.

I could speak no words to answer, to tell her of my sadness and regret.

So I swore a silent vow that I would get Greta back. I would haunt Baneswood until it spit out all those I loved. This I swore, if it cost me everything.

CHAPTER 17

We spent the next year trying to get back in.

Every day and every night, until it was all there was.

Igor gave the fence a gate, and men with axes poured through to cut down all the trees whose branches hung too close. They came at night when we couldn't hope to fight them and worked with their eyes on the moon.

Ulf robbed the men of their axes, when he could, and hacked at the fence until their blades dulled, until the thorns grew hard as metal and all the holes closed and we could not even see inside anymore. White scars covered Ulf's torso; his skin was a mass of them. But he was a man possessed. We all were.

"Where are they getting all the steel?" Ulf asked. Aurora sat beside him, her fingers laced with his, her arms empty of her child. He was the only one of us she didn't hate.

"They're trading with Sleepy Bramsville again," Gus said. "I saw a convoy. They have to replace the resources the woods once provided. The blacksmith must be working overtime."

"A new blacksmith, you mean." I still remembered the sight of the old one lying unmoving after Dag threw him into a house.

"So we attack a convoy," Dag said.

Gus shook his head. He looked older now, weathered and worn. "Convoys travel with an armed guard of twelve men. They fortify their position during the day and move only at night."

"How do they fortify their position?" I asked.

"They rest at a place where the trees grow so close together, we can't pass through in our wolf forms."

I closed my eyes, the frustration like a constant companion pounding behind my eyes.

"Show me where. I'll cut 'em down. These are our woods now. We won't leave places where we can't pass," Ulf said, and Gus nodded.

"They'll only find some other way of keeping their convoy safe," I said. It was hard to not feel defeated.

"I walked around to the far side today," Aurora said. Her voice was always quiet now, not bold like it had been before. "The fence is still moving. More and more of the forest is being swallowed. I bet they need the space to grow food inside and raise more animals."

"Shit," Dag said. The more self-sustaining the village became, the less chance we had.

Our meetings, held often at first, yielded nothing, and through the year, they became less and less frequent. Each of us settled into our new life in his own way.

Ulf grew resigned and lonely, though he was the only one Aurora could tolerate. They receded together into a pack that did not include the rest of us.

Dag was no longer Dag. He'd become a monster, inside and out. The curse, burrowing deep, had found the darkest secret in him and brought it forth. And the man who was the best of us became the worst.

Gus watched it all and couldn't fix it. The villagers stood at their sentry posts with hate in their hearts and torches in their hands; Aurora looked on her own brothers as enemies; Igor and Greta were right there on the other side of the wall; and he couldn't fix it.

As for me...well, in the end, I'd made the choice that doomed us all. I was a young man, but full of regret. My only hope for redemption was to fulfill my promise.

I spent my days in practice with my new body. Though I'd once thought the fence too high to jump, I now thought that I could make it, if I was willing to risk a few scars across my stomach.

At night, I built myself a runway.

"This is stupid," Dag said, watching, but I kept on anyway, and eventually Gus picked up a shovel, and Dag too. Ulf felled any trees in my way, and we made ourselves a hill. A hill to leap from.

When it was finished, months had passed. I'd grown a beard and wore it without care for how I looked. Dag had shaved his head and wore only furs to cover his muscular human form. Gus had lines around his eyes. He hung close to his twin and spoke less than before. And Ulf...strangely enough, Ulf was coming to life. Forced into a form he was afraid of, forced to live in it every day, he had ceased to be afraid.

I hoped that perhaps, this miracle might turn back the curse, but it did not. There was no escaping the curse now except to break it.

I fantasized about it at night, of course. In my vision, I went to the sorcerer as a wolf and threatened him, and he cowered and clutched his tooth and turned things back. Time itself rolled away and I was just a boy again, kicking my leg as I sat on a branch eating fruit and looking down at the townsfolk who came to sell wares at the market.

But I kept this impossible vision to my dreaming time. My priorities were clear.

Get Greta back. I'd promised.

Aurora came to see my runway before dawn on the day I meant to use it. She stood with me, her hard eyes staring up at the barrier that kept her from her daughter. She wore leathers that Dag had made for her from the animals he killed. The iron rod had never left her spine. During the day, when she slept, she had nightmares, and the birds avoided the tree house because of her screams.

"I'll go with you. I'll get on your back."

"You might fall off. And besides, I don't even know if I can make it." I tilted my head up to assess my obstacle, and Aurora did the same.

"You might just slam your face into the thorns and die," she said without emotion.

"Yes."

Aurora nodded up and down, up and down, lost in

thought.

In our first days in the woods, she'd spent all her time peering through the holes in the fence, trying to catch a glimpse of Greta on the streets. Only once, she had. She'd screamed and screamed until she had no voice. She'd pressed her face to the thorns, and she had a long thin scar along her cheek now. Greta had not heard.

"Rune."

"Yes?"

"If you can't get her out…"

I waited. My memory flashed back to the day we picked berries in the woods, before Igor came to town. Aurora's eyes had danced with blue light. There was joy in her laugh. She was a serious young mother and a hopeful young woman, and all of that was gone now, all of it.

"If you can't get her out, don't come back." She said this, too, without emotion, and I only nodded, accepting it as fair.

She walked away, and I turned to watch her leave, thinking this might be the last time I ever saw her. The thought didn't hurt like it once had. I'd suffered too many losses to fear one more.

"Aurora," I called after anyway.

She stopped walking but did not turn around.

"I did it because I love you. I was trying to save you."

She turned back around, and a sneer curled her lip.

"You did it because you need me. You always made me take care of you, of the whole family. You couldn't do without me, so you chose for me. You put what mattered to you over what mattered to me. And I'll never forgive you, Rune. Whatever you do today or any day after, I won't forgive you."

I leapt the wall. Thorns grazed my stomach like sharp fingernails, but they did not scratch deep. Elated, blood pumping, I landed hard on my paws in the streets of Baneswood.

I did not know where I was. The woods that once grew here had become fields planted with corn stalks and pastures where chickens roamed and clucked. At the sight of me, they startled, and I wondered if a chicken keeper would come running to see what spooked them.

Moving quietly, I hurried away.

This time, I had a plan, a plan I'd hatched over the course of months. A plan so simple, it was practically stupid.

I hugged the fence, staying out of the village proper. I circled it until I recognized Marius' fields. I snuck into Cat's barn. The sheep were gone. I curled up in a ball and lay down, ears alert. My large ears could hear her wake up in her house. I could hear when she left.

Where did she go? She'd been a huntress, and now she was barred from the woods. What did she do each day inside Igor's prison?

I waited silently, even when I heard her come home. I waited until dark when I became a man again. I put on her father's old coat, which hung on a wooden peg, and I walked through the dusk to her bedroom window. I knocked on her shutters.

Rap, rap.

Would she be angry still? Would she slam the shutters in my face when she saw it was me?

The shutters flew open and her eyes targeted me.

"Rune," she breathed, and threw herself half out the

window to hug me.

"Shh," I said, but I hugged her back. I hugged her like nobody had hugged me or loved me in months.

She got right down to business. "Greta. She's still living with him. He's raising her like his own daughter. It's sick to watch him buy her cream pops at the market, but he hasn't harmed her. And I don't think she's under a spell. Each day he drops her off at Clarissa's for daycare and picks her up before dinnertime."

I breathed out a deep sigh of relief. I knew Cat would come through for me.

"Thank you," I said into her neck, not letting go. If anything, I squeezed her tighter. "I missed you."

"I missed you too, Rune. Is Aurora okay?"

Reluctantly, I pulled away. "She's alive. She hates me, which is fair."

Cat's eyes hardened. "Dag?"

"He's…" I drifted off. She'd seen for herself how he was when he ripped apart her father. "He's gone," I finished.

"There was always anger in him," Cat said, "but he didn't let it control him before."

"The curse. It—"

Cat shook her head, vehemently rejecting my attempt to excuse away Dag's violence. "You were cursed too, Rune, and you're still a good man."

"It depends who you ask. Ask Aurora, she'll tell you I'm the worst of us."

Cat sighed and peered into my yellow eyes with her soulful ones. "Look, Rune, maybe I don't know you anymore. You've all changed so much. I've changed too. Baneswood…" she shuddered, "is not how it was. The animals left. The people are careful, hateful. The apothecary grows in power. He rules us.

"But here you are, still risking your life to try to get Greta away from him. When I look at you, I see something good that's still left in this world. I still see a good man."

The emotions moved through me like a river washing me clean. Gratitude, and a kind of relief, followed by a strange feeling of being humbled. I needed to be seen this way, seen as something other than a monster.

Then she said the words I longed to hear.

"Take me back with you," she whispered. Our hands clung to each other, resting on the sill. "I want to leave this place."

"I'm not who I was," I said quietly. "I climb trees to invade rather than escape. I pick berries to make poison. I'm lonely and sorry all the time."

I was trying to prepare her. The forest was not the magical fairyland she remembered, and I was not the boy she'd known.

"The whole world has changed," Cat said. "Not just you. I live in a cage. I have no family left but yours. I open my shutters and there are no birds singing on the other side. I want to be with the people I love. I want freedom."

"You could've come to us," I murmured. "Joined one of the parties that goes out and snuck away."

She smiled sadly. "And if I had, how would you get Greta?"

"You stayed because you knew I'd come back."

"One of you. For Greta. I had to be here to help you."

Hot and cold surges in my blood, and I knew what I'd always known anyway, which was that she was the most marvelous woman alive.

"If you're sure, Cat, I'll take you when I go. Of course I'll take you."

Her hand trailed down my face, and she smiled, sad but sure. "Thank you, Rune."

It was really I who owed her thanks. More than I could say. So I said nothing, and we jumped into discussion of how we'd get Greta back.

"Clarissa lets the kids play outside, and she doesn't watch them that carefully. After all, there's a giant fence. Who's going to take them? Where could they go? I'll lure Greta away and bring her back here. Then we just walk out the gate."

"You, Greta, and a wolf just walking down the street."

"Not much choice. Igor will know very quickly that Greta is gone."

"And you think they'll just let us out."

"Of course not. You'll slam your way through. The gate is the weak point in the fence. They cut a thousand-year-old oak to make doors that are a foot thick, but they're not ready yet. I think if you run into the current gate as hard as you can, you probably can crack it." She looked hesitant, apologetic. "Or you'll just smash your face. And there'll be men there protecting it." She huffed out. "I'm sorry. It's not a great plan."

"It is," I assured her. "It's going to work."

The next morning, Cat went to collect Greta while I anxiously stood at attention in her barn, taking up the whole space, unable to pace. A cage of walls and anticipation.

Noises approached and my heart roared so loudly that even my huge ears could barely discern if it was enemy or friend until I heard a toddler's laugh. Then relief flooded me, followed by determination. The next bit would be hardest. Cat rounded the door and came into sight with Greta.

Greta was walking. My heart broke for Aurora, who would never see her daughter's first steps. Greta's blond hair, pale as dandelion fluff, curled around her flushed face like a halo. When she saw me, she hiccuped and began to whimper.

Instantly, I lay down, and Cat gathered Greta into her arms and said, "Shh. It's a dog, see? A really big dog. There's no need to be afraid. Do you want to pet his nose?"

Together, they came forward until Greta's little palm was patting my wet black nose, and I was trying not to sneeze because it tickled.

We walked to the gate. It was not far, but my heart pounded. People would see us. They would come. *He* would come. Cat picked up Greta and carried her, walking quickly. She wore her leathers, and her bow was over her shoulder along with a backpack.

The first scream. Pottery shattered. A villager went running.

We broke into a run.

There were only two men at the gate. They barely defended this side, as Cat had promised. I picked up speed. Now I was grateful for the conditioning I'd put my body through these past months. My legs rocketed over streets and past houses. I ran until I was just a blur, and I slammed my entire body into the gate. I felt it shudder, and a crack ran through the wood.

Elation!

The men swung their axes, but I jumped away and circled back. I spun around and slammed myself into the gate once more. The iron bar buckled, and the crack widened. Once more, perhaps just once more. I only needed a hole big enough for a little girl and a woman. After that, who cared?

An axe sliced my skin. I took the weapon from the wielder and threw the other man against the fence.

Cat was there. She bounced Greta and hid her face so that she could not see what I did and become afraid. Cat's eyes were worried, darting every way.

I wheeled around to attack the gate one more time, but *he* was there, strolling down the street in his garish blue and yellow, a sick full smile plastered to his face. He held out his arms in welcome. "You came back. I knew you would. What took you so long?"

He looked utterly unworried, but I looked closer and it was a farce. His army had not yet arrived, and Greta was not with him to serve as a shield. His hand moved to the talisman at his neck, but he could not stop me with it. I could leap to him and close my teeth around his heart and feel the warm iron taste of his blood spurt out onto my tongue. His life force would pump into me, and he would crumble. The curse would break; the hate would leave the hearts of the villagers; Greta and I would walk away free.

Maybe.

Or maybe Igor would trick me again, and Aurora would never get her daughter back.

I turned from revenge. I set my eyes on the gate and I raced forward once more, throwing every ounce of my weight against the doors. Slam! And shove, shove. The iron creaked and whined as it bent. The wood thundered as it splintered. The hinges tore from the fence posts, and the doors fell open.

I barked. *Go! Go!*

Cat raced out the opening, her boots pounding against the

ground, Greta clutched tightly against her chest. I saw Aurora run out from the trees to crash into them, grabbing at her daughter, sobbing. They disappeared into the woods.

Behind me, the sorcerer muttered. Vines uncoiled like poisonous snakes, crawling to close the opening.

Another choice yawned before me.

Kill Igor, or follow Cat out while I still could.

I knew what Dag would do. Probably Gus and Aurora would even do the same.

But I was done making monstrous choices. I was not a monster just because he'd shaped me like one.

My family waited in the woods, and my window was closing. I turned away from the pull of revenge, from the hope of a curse broken. I ran out to join my family. The gate closed behind me, and I was forever barred.

As soon as night fell and I could speak, I sought out Cat. She sat in our tree house, which Aurora had made her home.

"This is much more comfortable than it once was," she said, smiling. Tension had eased in her shoulders and she cocked her head, listening to the night sounds of the forest.

I sat beside her, knees to chest. "Thank you for today. I can never repay you for what you did."

She shrugged and reached into the backpack she'd brought. She lifted something out. Even in the dim moonlight I could see it was leather of the most brilliant red color I'd ever seen.

"It's beautiful," I said, entranced. I unfolded it. It was a jacket of deer leather, with bronze buttons. In certain areas, the leather had turned a red so deep, it was almost purple. In others, a creamy orange like fresh peaches.

She smiled, pleased, and nudged me with her shoulder. "I made it for you. You said to make you something. Aurora gave me her dye. That night you came, I only gave you one vial."

"I'm honored." I caressed the leather. Color like the sunset.

Cat took my hand. She squeezed. "What I'm trying to say is...I knew you'd be back. I knew you'd come back for me. I didn't give up hope."

This was not the end of our story. We lived long lives, each of us, and what we did went down in legend and then was forgotten, as real lives generally are.

Aurora took Greta and went deep into the woods to a place where Ulf had not felled the trees. With that choice, she banished us from her life. She raised her daughter alone, in peace, and allowed only Cat to visit.

Ulf made himself a home, and Gus and Dag joined him there. In the years that followed, young women with wild hearts and free minds sometimes found a way to get out of Baneswood. When they did, they found us, and there were pups and sometimes joy, and our family grew.

As for Cat and I, well, I married her. I carved her a ring from the wood of our tree house tree, and we said our vows with all our family as witness.

But of course the war raged on. We found new ways past Igor's defenses and Baneswood found new ways to keep us out. And on and on, through time. When I had pups of my own, I told them the story of it all, even though it's a terrible story, isn't it? Grim as they come, and it should never be told.

THE END

THE STORY CONTINUES IN
THE WOODS...

Hundreds of years after the sorcerer's curse, sheltered Red lives in terror of the wolves who haunt the Woods outside her walled village. Only the Huntsmen—an army of ax-wielding warriors led by Red's legendary Gran—are allowed outside, and Red is no warrior. She dreams of freedoms she can't imagine, but the village is her trap.

Until a brutal attack leaves Gran on the edge of death. To save her, Red must brave the Woods alone.

The beasts drive her deep into the shadows of an unexpected hidden world, where old loyalties are called into question and ancient secrets are revealed. Now Red must choose whether to turn her back on her home to embrace a new love she couldn't have seen coming. For she never expected she could love a beast.

Use the QR code to get your copy of this dark Little Red Riding Hood retelling now!

Thank you for reading Rune's story,
and learning the truth about the origin of the
monsters who haunt the Woods.

Help other readers find this book by writing a
review to share with them what your reading
experience was like.

WANT MORE TO READ?

Trapped and alone in a blizzard in the deep Woods, eleven-year-old Selma makes a deal to save her mother's life.
But every deal comes with a cost.

Discover the whole story in *The Winter Stags*.
Sign up for Em McDermott's newsletter to receive this short story as a free gift.

To get your copy, visit:
https://stories.emmcdermott.com/free

Acknowledgments

A big thank you to my team of beta readers: Emmeline, TaniaRina, Juliana, Debbie, Rachel, Julia, and Rebecca. My goal is to write a story that readers will love, and you guys let me know if I'm on the right track. Several of you also wrote reviews and alerted me of typos and grammar issues, for which I am eternally grateful. Thank you!

Also, a grateful acknowledgment of my trusty critique partner, Jenny. You're the best!

About the Author

Em McDermott writes every day in a tiny cabin in the woods of upstate New York, where the walls are lined with bookcases brimming with novels and fairy statues. She considers ancient myths and fairy tales to be the world's oldest fantasy stories, and elements from these tales appear in all her work. Em shares her home with her two loving partners, a small flock of dragons (cough, cough, pet chickens), and more zucchini plants than is entirely reasonable.

Em writes fairy tale fantasy and epic fantasy. Her stories are dark but are ultimately hopeful adventures of human love and transformation. You can read some of them for free by signing up for her newsletter at:

https://stories.emmcdermott.com/free.

Get in contact with Em on social media or on her website, emmcdermott.com. She loves building relationships with her readers.

Facebook.com/emmcdermotts